# BDSM at the Enema Lounge
## (Complete Series)

## &

# Back Room BDSM
## (Complete Series)

By Sarah Hung

# BDSM at the Enema Lounge

## #1: Ass Stretching, Gangbang, and Enema BDSM Party

Kiley made her way through the supermarket slowly, looking at the things around her as if contemplating shopping, delaying the moment she would let go, savoring the fear of strangers staring as she exposed herself for all to see. One of the workers watched her for a moment as if she were about to steal, headed over to her, and asked, "Was there anything you needed help with tonight, Kiley?"

Kiley was taken aback by the use of her name. The man, who happened to be well-chiseled and probably a few years younger than her, perhaps barely legal, smiled at her widely and nodded his head. "It's okay. I'm here to collect you, assuming you still want to be collected."

"I see," Kiley mumbled. "I do." Her nerves were obvious, and sensing this, the young man smiled at her again and offered his hand.

"Nothing horrible is going to happen. I'll personally make sure of it." Kiley took his hand and followed him toward the back of the store. Passing the electronics, the baby goods, the shoes, the automotive section, and into a little door reading, "Employees only."

Once in this backroom, Kiley's grip on the stranger's hand tightened as they continued through a warehouse of items waited to be stocked, and ended up at another door. The young, buff worker took his time getting the key out of his pocket and opening the door.

Inside, Kiley saw a number of people relaxing around a couch. In one corner was a cart full of different devices and instruments that Kiley couldn't quite make out. As her usher went to walk forward, Kiley stopped in her tracks.

"You don't have to be here," he assured her once more. "But we are happy to see you." There must have been at least ten men and a few women, but all of them were staring directly at Kiley now as she hesitated.

Kiley nodded and walked forward into the room. Hesitantly, she let go of her usher's hand, and watched him intently as he moved off, apparently in search of someone that wasn't in the room yet.

"Take a seat, honey," one of the women stood up and met her, leading her to the couch in the middle of the crowd, sitting down with her, and continuing to talk. "You are so beautiful," she cooed.

"T-thank you," Kiley responded, trying to focus on the woman and ignore those around her. "You are too." Kiley blushed hard, trembling a bit

The woman pet Kiley's face with the back of her hand. "So soft, and young, honey. You don't need to be nervous. Everyone will love you." The woman kissed on Kiley's neck. A few small woos and other affirmations emitted from the small crowd, and Kiley felt a shock of tingles from her head to her toe. All of a sudden, her pussy was gushing with fluids as the woman continued to loosen her up, kissing up her neck some more before kissing her on the mouth.

"If you'd be more comfortable, we can all get naked," one of the men shouted out. There were giggles.

The woman shot the man a flirty glance, and unbuttoned her own top, showing her bare breasts. "Your turn, sweetie," the woman said to Kiley.

Kiley fumbled with her top, unbuttoning herself

slowly, revealing her lacy black bra holding her C-cups in their captivity. The woman kissed her chest, forced the shirt the rest of the way off, and popped her bra. When Kiley's breasts fell out, everyone cheered. Looking around, Kiley could see the men all had erections. The couple women still seated with everyone else where rubbing the men, and themselves, and there was an understanding in the room that it was time for shirts off.

The woman loosening up Kiley took one of her breasts, sucking hard on the nipple before swapping to the next. Kiley bright red face flushed with heat, her vagina quivering in her panties as the woman's hand made its way to her zipper, pulling it down while never disconnecting from her titties.

Kiley reached out and groped the woman's breast quickly, but pulled back, unsure of herself and her role in this event.

"That's it, enjoy yourself, Kiley," the woman said, pushing her down and pulling down Kiley's pants before mounting her and forcing her titties into Kiley's face. Kiley took the moment to grope, suck, and lick on the woman's titties. She touched the woman's bear skin, and felt herself completely lost in the moment. Almost without noticing, she'd been stripped of her panties and was laying there naked, petting another woman as a small crowd continued to watch her. The woman dropped down between her legs, and sucked Kiley's clit deep into her mouth, flicking it hard with her tongue. Kiley shook almost instantly with an orgasm, incapable of holding back. The woman did not stop, though, and continued to eat her out, finger bang her, and send her writhing. Just as Kiley thought she would explode again, the woman backed off, wiped her face, and joined the crowd.

"Kiley," a new stranger said, standing with the young man who had ushered her into this strange room.

Kiley laid there exposed, dripping from her cunt, re-alizing now that almost everyone in the room was nearly naked, the woman she'd been fooling around with now kissing another woman, sharing her taste between each other's lips.

Above her stood the new stranger, a dark woman with cold eyes. "I hope you enjoyed that. I hope you're ready for your punishments." She diverted her attention to the woman who had been pleasuring Ki-ley, "You too." Sheepishly, the adventurous woman joined Kiley once again on the couch.

"You," the woman said to her young man, "ready everything, fetch the cart." He obligingly went to cart and seemed to be setting things up.

"You eat her, it's only fair," the woman instructed Kiley to taste her first bit of pussy. Kiley happily obliged, frightened by the presence of the obvious leader in the group, but hungry to tear away the woman's panties and dive deep into her short bush and breath in the fragrance of the woman's excitements. As Kiley started in gingerly, the woman grabbed her hair and pushed her hard into her snatch, grinding heavily, going full-sprint toward an orgasm, knowing that time was precious in the duration it would take the young man to prepare everything. Kiley's tongue work was obviously amateurish, but just the opportunity to ride her face was enough to get the last of the woman's juices flowing. As she began to shake hard with an orgasm, the dark, cold woman slapped her across the face. The initial gasp sounded painful, but immediately another gasp of pleasure sounded out behind it, and another, and another, until the woman lay there spent, Kiley's face covered in her goosh.

The crowd clapped respectfully and the mistress bowed to them all while gesturing to the women. "Kiley and Veronica, everyone. They are going to be our stars tonight, and I welcome you all to take out your dicks, flick those peas, and find the balance between pleasure and pain that works best for you. Tonight, you control yourselves. Tomorrow, you may be up here, under my control. As you know, this will be an interactive event, so don't get too excited yet."

"It's all ready," the young man said, wheeling up the cart. Kiley's face went white. She knew what was about to happen, but the reality of the moment set in once more.

"I am Mistress Eva," the dark woman said. "What will you call me at all times?"

"Mistress Eva," Veronica responded quickly.

"Mistress… Eva…" Kiley hesitated.

"On your needs, asses up in the air and toward the crowd."

The women assumed the position. Mistress Eva adjusted the cart beside the couch, in just the right position to be out of view of all the guests. She rubbed her hand over each of the women's asses, smacked them playfully a few times, and bowed to the audience once more.

A few of the men had their dicks out, in their hands, stroking at a pace meant to prolong their ejaculation. The couple women were taking turns sucking a cock, stroking a cock, eating each other. The entire room reeked of sex and anticipation.

"V. first," Eva motioned to her young man, who immediately took a bottle of lube to Veronica's asshole, dropping a few drops on, before returning to the cart and bringing out a butt plug. Without much warning, he shoved it deep inside of Veronica, who let out a screech, but whose pussy could visibly be seen leaking at the fullness in her asshole. The young man pulled the plug out, pushed it back in, and pulled it out. He left it there, and went to Kiley. When he dropped a little lube on her asshole, she had a knee-jerk reaction, almost pulling away.

Kiley's white skin looked like porcelain, and this time as the young man used another plug, he was easy and gentle on her, knowing it to be her first time. "This isn't daycare, boy," Eva said. "Shove it in there."

He obliged, leaning down to Kiley's ear and apologizing as she let out a curdling yelp at the abrupt intrusion. Yet, there was her pussy, wet and leaking just like Veronica's.

The Mistress approached the young man and Kiley, and dipped a finger into Kiley's spread open pussy. Taking it out of Kiley's slit, she offered her finger to her young man, who eagerly sucked it off her index finger, lingering a moment longer than necessary. "You may," was all Eva said before the young man stripped down to his bare skin, his 8" dick flopping out, hard and ready. Without much warning, in his eagerness, he slammed it deep inside of Kiley's open slit, the butt plug making it harder to get into the tight hole without completely splitting her open.

Kiley let out a heavy sigh, and as the man began to pump, the crowd's energy was apparent. More dicks in hands, more dicks in mouths, even a couple men pleasuring each other.

"Take turns on V," she instructed. Half the group instantly rose to their feet, and formed a line behind Veronica, each taking one minute turns penetrating her cunt, smashing into her hard, pulling and pushing on the buttplug, slapping her ass until it was beet red. Three men and the two women remained on the couch, watching, and taking turns pleasuring each other. One of the women remained sandwiched between two men, one in her ass, one in her cunt, and would remain in this position for almost the rest of the evening, the men sometimes switching out with other men in the room. These were men that could control themselves...

As the young man pushed into Kiley's hole, greedily and violently stabbing at her inner walls, the men continued to take short turns on Veronica, nobody trying to explode or fill anybody up with cum just yet. Finally, as Veronica screamed out in ecstasy once more, the Mistress gently had everyone back off. No more sitting necessary. Kiley was close behind her, still only taking the dick of the younger man in the room, whose girth and length made her almost too full. After she writhed and screamed out in ecstasy, he pulled out, a pool of her juices flowing to the ground. Pulling himself together, the young man readied something on the cart as the mistress had everyone stand back. She popped the butt plug from Veronica's ass, pushed her over, and let her lay on one side of the long couch, clearly spent, needing a bit of rest.

"Are you ready for the main event?" Mistress whispered into Kiley's ears.

"Yes, Mistress Eva," she cooed, dizzy with the events going on around her.

The mistress removed the plug from Kiley's ass, and immediately afterwards her young man shoved a tube inside. Attached to the tube was a bag of liquid. The young man aimed Kiley's ass toward the crowd, and slowly lifted the bag to begin filling her asshole with the warm liquid. The immediate sensation of being just short of bursting filled Kiley with panic. As the fluid kept pouring in, she held her breath for a moment, gasped for air, and held her breath again, clenching her cheeks together hard, trying not to spill out. The crowd cheered, still stroking themselves, the threesome still taking place, boners and juices and everything everywhere.

The fullness of the enema made Kiley shake and squirm and want to complain, but she didn't dare move more than a few inches. She knew she had no control left. And yet, for some reason, her pussy still leaked out, her groin still ached to get fucked again.

After a few minutes, the mistress nodded to her young man. He pulled the tube from Kiley's asshole, and told her there was a bucket just behind her whenever she was ready. The crowd silenced in this moment. Waiting for the stretched out hole to drop its entire load as they gathered around closer, the couples fucking finally standing still with the rest of the crowd.

As Kiley leaned herself back, the flow of fluid from her asshole ran down her legs, down her coochie, onto the couch, and finally most of it came out in one large gush, an audible spilling into the bucket. A couple of the men stood close by and shot their loads at the same time, shooting far enough that they went up Kiley's back, into her hair, and all over the couch. The other men held out for just a moment longer.

"Proceed," Mistress said. And with this, the young man wiped her up with a towel, mounted her asshole, pumped a few times, and deposited his huge load of cum deep inside her freshly enema-ed asshole. Shaking the last drops out, satisfied finally, he moved out of the way. The next man approached, shoved his dick in her pussy for just a few thrusts, and then placing the top of his penis at the absurdly stretched and gaping butthole, he deposited his load as well. They continued until every man had cum into her asshole, the warmth and fullness almost lost on Kiley, now in a daze from the experience.

All the while, Veronica had been lying on the couch, fucked silly and spent before, but slowly playing with herself now. The young man removed the bucket, and wiped down the area around Kiley, the mistresses instructing everyone to find a seat, and for motioning for Veronica.

"You're the bucket now," the Mistress said. In those few words, there was an excitement that Veronica couldn't contain. She quickly jumped to her feet, placed herself below Kiley's raised asshole, and had her mouth wide open. The mistress pushed Kiley's back down gently, instructing her to let the jizz spill out of her asshole, down Veronica's face, into her mouth, sticking in her eyes, covering her tits. Veronica, mouth open, tried to suck down as much of it as she could, and without any instruction, shoved her face to Kiley's gaping hole and sucked hard to get every last drop she could. When she was satisfied that no more would come out, she pushed Kiley onto the couch, mounted her, and began kissing her hard. Kiley kissed back, but was in a daze.

The crowd remained quietly watching, all spent and happy and feeling disgusting about themselves in the best possible ways. The mistress left without another word, leaving her young man to take care of all the cleanup duties and deciding when the night would truly be over.

## #2: Big Black Slave Dick, Butt-plugged Enema for the New Girl, and Double Penetration

When Kiley woke up in a daze, it only took finding Veronica in bed next to her to remember the events of the night before. The enema. The crowd. The men filling her asshole up with their jizz and then Veronica swallowing it and sucking it out. It all seemed so surreal, but here was Veronica sleeping in her bed next to her, still stinking of jizz and sex, completely naked, and looking beautiful.

"Good morning," Veronica rolled over, wrapping her arm around Kiley.

"G-good morning," Kiley stuttered. "I... do you want breakfast."

"I'd love some, but I probably need to go home and get ready for work," Veronica cupped one of Kiley's breasts. "I don't know if I'll have enough time to..."

Without finishing her sentence, Veronica continued to grope Kiley's tits, and then kiss on her bare neck for a moment. Kiley felt chills roll up her spine as Veronica's hand wandered to her bare pussy, still sticky and dirty from the night before. Massaging her clit, Veronica buried her face into Kiley's boobs, rubbing hard against them as if she were a cat trying to get pets.

"Let's go to the shower," Veronica said, hopping up, basically yanking Kiley along with her. Traipsing through the apartment, over a pile of clothes from the night before, and entering the shower, Veronica took the offensive once more, pushing Kiley against the wall just mere seconds after the hot water started to wash away the grit from the night before. Finger-banging her with two fingers, Kiley's soppy wet cunt flowed freely, Kiley's eyes rolling back in her head as her newfound friend continued to fondle her. As Kiley felt herself losing grip on reality further, Veronica dropped to her knees and slammed her mouth hard against her cunt, nibbling at her clit, her fingers still pounding into her slit. Kiley let out a loud moan, began to shake, and almost tried pushing Veronica away as the orgasm intensified and her juices flowed and mingled with the water. When Veronica finally pulled away, Kiley reached for Veronica's body. Veronica kissed her hard on the mouth and hopped out of the shower.

"I hate to eat and run," Veronica chuckled at herself, "but I have to get going! I'll be by later tonight to pick you up."

Kiley hadn't actually considered if she wanted to return to "The Enema Lounge," as she'd nicknamed it in her head, but she confirmed with a nod that she would be around for Veronica. As Veronica disappeared into Kiley's apartment, Kiley lathered herself up with soap and began to clean herself up.

###

As nighttime came, Kiley sat on her couch, nervous and excited for the events that had taken place and that were going to take place again. When the bell rang, Kiley answered the door to see Veronica with a stranger in tow. This stranger was a tall, black hunk whose large package could be seen half-erect in his gym shorts. Kiley felt a tingle in her panties.

"Are you ready?" Veronica asked. "Jerome is coming with us tonight. I hope you don't mind."

"Not at all," Kiley stammered, trying not to look at his package.

Cramming into the back of a taxi, Veronica directed the driver to head toward the supermarket where the backroom club was located. Without provocation, Jerome sat between the women and rested a hand on each of their exposed thighs, lightly caressing them both. He had said almost nothing, but he didn't seem the least bit shy about his chubby member being half-erect or his willingness to slip a digit into Kiley's skirt to rub her clit a bit. Veronica absentmindedly stroked his cock for the entire ride, and Kiley tried to remain calm as she watched it growing to a huge 12 inches.

Once at the supermarket, they made their way together toward the same backroom they had previously visited, where Kiley was the show for all to see the night before. She had no idea of the intentions for her tonight, but she had a feeling Jerome would be playing an important role in the events. Entering the longue, they were greeted by Mistress Eva's young man, whose name still eluded most the patrons. He welcomed them in and told them to take a seat anywhere they would like, to do as they please, but not to get too excited or spent before the events actually began.

In the room were several of the same men from the night before. Others appeared to be newcomers, and tonight there were almost as many women, none of them the same women Kiley had previously seen in the establishment other than Veronica. The men all had boners, and the women were mostly naked already, some of them touching themselves or getting touched by others. Kiley hoped to blend in tonight instead of be on show, but having never officially agreed with the Mistress that she'd be showing up again, she wasn't sure what was in store or why she so blindly agreed to follow Veronica. What she did know is that these people had fetishes, enemas being one of their favorites.

When the young man left, Kiley knew it was to fetch the mistress. Upon their entrance, Mistress Eva carried a whip, and the young man pushed a cart with a bucket, several chains, and a number of other instruments Kiley couldn't quite make out. Kiley felt nervous, unsure of her role in the evening still.

"Thank you all for coming," the mistress said, silencing the room immediately, stopping the small amounts of foreplay from continuing for the duration of her introductions. "For everyone that came out last night, I trust that we made it a memorable experience for our newest woman. Everyone please give a round of applause for Kiley."

The room cheered, even those that hadn't been there, and Kiley felt herself blush and heat up immediately.

"As you all understand, I am your mistress. I am the one calling the shots, and at any point you feel inclined to disagree with what I ask of you, you shall leave and never return to another event. That said, we have the safety of each of you in mind, and I encourage you to take advantage of these very special evenings together. For tonight, Veronica has brought us a special guest and we have a new lady joining our ranks. It will be a special night indeed."

Jerome stood and moved to the front of the room, near the mistress, near her young man. His member protruded from beneath his gym shorts, and the room of women marveled at the size and girth apparent from the outline it created. The Mistress, with no warning, slapped her small whip across his back and screamed, "Drop the shorts!"

Jerome seemed almost unmoved by the pain, dropped his shorts, and removed his shirt to show a back full of whip scars. He was not new to the events going on around him. The young man who blindly followed the mistress took the chains from the cart and proceeded to attach a clasp around Jerome's neck, which he then connected to a small piece on the floor.

"Jerome is everyone's slave tonight. Regardless of what else we have in store, he will be right here for anyone and everyone to do what they please. Ladies, that means you. But first, we have a new girl here to initiate, so please stay tuned for the audience interaction."

The young man pulled a small girl from the corner where she was hiding. She looked timid and uncomfortable, but willingly followed him to the couch, pushed just to the side of Jerome. Mistress Eva lightly smacked the girl on the ass with the whip, motioning for her to strip. When she didn't understand the command, the young man popped open the button of her jean shorts and yanked them down to reveal she wasn't wearing any panties. She was visibly wet, and the crowd's small cheer indicated that they were excited. The crowd began to molest each other more, women stroking the men, men fingering the women, all still fixing their gazes on the chained up mandingo and the small white girl who was now face first on the couch, her small ass in the air.

"Slave!" Mistress Eva screamed, no longer welcoming or even addressing the crowd. "Spit on this girl's asshole."

He obliged, spitting on her asshole, the young man following behind him with a small butt plug that he worked into her ass as she let out yelps of pain. The slave, Jerome, stood nearby, his dick rock hard. When Mistress Eva whipped him across the back, he stepped forward and tugged out the butt plug and pushed it back in, the small girl's pussy emitting just the smallest amount of fluids. He licked his hand and rubbed it across his cock. The girl, a mere five foot tall, petite, almost smaller around than his dick, was to be skewered by this huge black man's cock. Without much warning he placed it against the tiny opening of her cunt and pushed into her very hard. She let out a loud scream, and the crowd's energy immediately ramped up. They began more aggressively fondling one another, one of the women taking a dick already while still stroking another man.

As Jerome pushed his huge member into the little woman, she continued to let out gasps of pain and pleasure until finally she was loose enough to fully enjoy the moment. It wasn't long before she screamed out in a blood-curdling orgasm, shaking, and begging him to go faster and harder as she rode the wave. Not quite done with her orgasm, he yanked out her butt plug, eliciting another loud scream, and pulled his dick out and shoved it all the way down her ass in almost a single movement. The curdling scream from her throat followed quickly by a whimpering and shaking that few had ever seen. She collapsed on the couch, twitching, her fluids drenching the couch and the floor below it. Jerome made a few more pumps before pulling out and returning to his spot as everyone's slave. With this, the women in the room understood that Jerome was now available.

Veronica quickly grabbed Kiley's hand and led her over to Jerome, basically pushing her onto her knees in front of him and taking the lead in cleaning the new girl's asshole and pussy off his dick with her mouth. Kiley joined in, the two of them having plenty of room to lick, suck, and nibble the huge black dick like a corn cob. Other women stood nearby, fondling themselves and each other, waiting for their turns.

On the couch, the young man once again lifted the girl's ass in the air, and with a tube in one hand and a bag in another, he positioned the bucket beneath her. Several of the men had migrated to be closer to this action, stroking themselves as the woman squirmed with the liquid filling her asshole. Once full of fluid, the young man once again popped the butt plug into her, a gush of the saline solution coming out in the process. The first of several men took his place in the line, pushing his dick into the small woman with the fluid still inside her, seeping out the edges of the plug, waiting to explode. It was perhaps a dangerous game of hot potato, but she held her ass as high in the air as possible to avoid any accidents. As the men took turns taking her on, she squirmed with the need to empty herself.

The Mistress stood back and watched her pawns. As a Mistress, she knew that she could be much harder on this lot, but letting them take care of their own desires almost always worked out for her own pleasure. She motioned her young man to her, her personal slave, and stroked his cock for just a moment. "Kiley," she said to him quietly.

Kiley and Veronica felt satiated having cleaned off

Jerome's dick, and now they've demanded that he fuck Kiley's dripping wet pussy. With her skirt on one of the seats, she bent over in front of him, taking his huge member as he pounded into her. Veronica lay beneath them, alternating between licking her clit and licking his balls. It didn't take long at all for Jerome to blow a huge load in her pussy, Veronica catching the drippings below. The other women looked upset for a moment, but as Kiley and Veronica moved away, the Mistress stepped in and told the other women to continue with him. And with that affirmation, it was clear that Jerome didn't need any recovery time.

Before Kiley could really realize what was happening, Veronica had left her side to stroke one of the men that were still watching the new girl try to hold in the fluids from the enema as several men took turns slowly pumping into her, small amounts of the solution leaking out with some of the harder thrusts. The man Veronica had grabbed seemed happy to take her to a couch instead of remaining in line, and soon Veronica was getting assfucked by another man after mounting the first.

Kiley, unsure of herself, saw that the Mistress and her young man were looking her way. The young man approached her and began to grope her softly. "The Mistress wants you to come alone tomorrow," he told her. "I don't know what she has in mind, but know that if you don't agree, you'll be asked not to join in anymore."

Kiley just nodded. She would have agreed without the warning. She felt him push his hard and warm member up close to her. "You will be fine, I promise." With this, Kiley reached her hand down and wrapped her fingers around his member, stroking it. He walked her to one of the chair, sat himself down, and nodded for her to do what she pleased. She first lowered her pussy over him, sliding her already cum-drenched pussy onto his 8" member and properly wetting it. Pulling away, she positioned her asshole over his cock and slowly sat down on it, pushing through any discomfort until his cock was buried completely inside of her. She rose and fell slowly, still watching the other events in the room... the women taking turns sucking and fucking Jerome, Veronica taking two dicks at once, the small new girl beginning to convulse with an orgasm...

As the new girl began to convulse, she could do nothing to maintain her composure, and it was only a mere second before the man currently plowing her vagina was able to step back as she nearly collapsed, trying so desperately to aim her ass toward the bucket. As the butt plug came flying out, so did all the fluid from the enema. Most of it splashed into the bucket, but everywhere around was also drenched.

24

The crowd let out a wild cheer as the girl whimpered and crawled into a ball on the couch. Kiley pushed her ass down against the young man harder and harder. Another woman joined in, clicking and finger-banging her pussy relentlessly, pushing her to orgasm, causing her to shake, convulse, and finally during her orgasm, her asshole squeezed the young man just right. He blew his load deep inside of her. As she lifted off his dick, his cum tumbled out all over his pubes, and the other woman began to lick him clean. Kiley felt full and satisfied and sleepy, ready only to go home, but realizing that the night was far from over as Veronica let out a piercing scream, shaking violently with a dick in her pussy and a dick in her ass, as the women began pairing off with men between sessions with Jerome. As the Mistress took stock over her minions, a man nursed the new girl back into action and buried his dick deep inside her asshole.

Kiley joined the line for Jerome once more, pondering on what the Mistress wanted with her in private, enjoying the night, and uncertain of where all of this would head.

## #3: Handcuffed, Gagged, Electrocuted, and Penetrated by the Tranny Mistress and Her Slave

Kiley woke up to an empty apartment. Veronica had spent the night again, but must have slipped out early in the morning. Thinking back on the raucous from the night before, Kiley felt herself get wet all over again at the thought of all the debauchery… fucking Jerome, the new girl and the enema, Veronica getting double penetrated, sitting on the Mistress' boy's cock until it was so deep in her asshole she could barely think straight. Was this going to be her life now? What did the Mistress have in store for her that night?

Shaking the thoughts of wild sex parties and her own newfound sluttiness, Kiley showered, dressed herself for work, and left home feeling somehow different than the last time she'd seen any of her day-to-day acquaintances. Would they be able to smell the change in her? Would they know? Do they have secret lives too?

Arriving at work, Kiley entered the building with a newfound hatred for the mundane and boring life she'd allowed herself to build. She worked at a desk, mostly answering phone calls and emails for people that wanted something, sometimes addressing larger clients as they came in to meet with the CEOs or sales reps or whoever. Working for a supplier of office supplies did nothing for her. The pay wasn't even that great.

Sitting down and unloading her things, one of her co-workers followed behind her through the door and greeted her with a friendly smile.

"How was your weekend?" he said sheepishly, leaning against the front desk and staring hard at Kiley.

"It was boring," Kiley answered back. "But nothing to complain about." She felt herself tingle at the lie, knowing she'd had more sex in the last two days than the five years combined.

"Any hot dates?"

"I had a woman sleep over," Kiley whispered to him, almost jokingly.

Her colleague laughed at the idea. "Yeah? You don't seem like a carpet muncher to me."

"Devon!" an older black woman slapped him as she walked by. "Shut yo mouth."

"Did you have any hot dates?" Kiley asked back.

Devon laughed again, and then hunkered closer to whisper. "I tried to, but this girl just wanted some standard dinner and movie night..." he paused to consider his next words. "Which would be fine, but we've been out on five dates already."

"Maybe she's just in it for the free stuff."

"I should just date someone like you," he laughed again. "Might get to have a threesome with two women!"

"Devon!" the old black lady screamed from across the room.

"You might," Kiley winked at him. "But I don't know that you could handle it."

Devon's face flushed red. He had, on several occasions, been inappropriate towards Kiley. This was the first time she'd done so back, at least so blatantly. He felt his dick lurch in his pants a little. "If you want to put me to the test, please let me know."

As the day progressed, Kiley fought hard to keep her mind off the fact that Mistress Eva had specifically asked her to come by "The Enema Lounge" alone that night. Her thoughts raced from enemas to lashings to getting tied up and tortured for days, but she knew that no matter the events, she would be showing up.

###

After work, Kiley returned to the supermarket whose backrooms included a secret sex lounge. Once inside the room where every nasty occurrence happened, she found it completely empty. There were no longer couches, no longer a cart of sex toys, nobody was around at all. An employee walked by and stopped her.

"Ma'am, this is staff only," he said to her.

Kiley didn't know what to think. She knew that the Mistress told her to arrive here, and she didn't want to leave so quickly should she show up soon after this annoying encounter.

"I'm supposed to meet…" Kiley started. The employee walked close to her.

"Ma'am, you have to leave the warehouse area. I really don't give a shit, but it's a liability, and I'm the one on shift."

Kiley groped his arm sensually, "Can I just stay for a couple more minutes? Then I'll be gone."

The man looked her up and down, thought about what she must look like beneath her clothes, but reached for his walkie-talkie anyway. "Security…" his voice trailed off in Kiley's head. She wasn't going to meet the mistress after all. Within moments security was dragging her out of the warehouse area and into their small security headquarters. There were two guards, both of them young and fit. One seemed a little less aggressive than the other, telling the other that Kiley was no harm, and he could go back to watching the cameras.

As the one security guard walked out, the remaining guard offered Kiley a seat. "I have to process you," he said. "This doesn't really mean anything, I just need to take your picture, write out the incident, and then you'll be free to go."

Kiley nodded, agitated by the turn of events. "Sure, whatever," she mumbled. "I wasn't doing anything."

"I know," he said calmly. "It's just policy. You can simply leave now if you wish, but we're supposed to ban you from the store completely if you do that."

"No, it's fine," Kiley said. "Just take the picture."

The guard set up a large camera directly in front of Kiley. It seemed abnormally large considering a digital camera could be so much simpler and quicker for their purposes, but she fixed her hair quickly, and gave it the biggest smile she could.

"Say cheese," the guard said.

Before Kiley could say anything, the flash went off, bright as the sun crashing onto the earth, blinding her completely for a moment. Within that split second she felt a bag wrapped around her head, around her face, and felt herself getting dragged out of the room to fuck knows where. Kicking and screaming, Kiley fought to no avail as four strong arms carried her away.

"WHAT THE FUCK!" she screamed. "LET ME GO!"

But it was no use. When they deposited her on what felt like a mattress, she felt cuffs quickly clasped to her wrists, heard a loud clang of the cuffs hooked to the bedframe, and then the sound of feet walking away slowly. She continued to scream out for a moment before hearing another set of steps.

"Hey! Hey! Let me out of here!"

"Sweetie," a voice said. It was raspy, deep and menacing, unfamiliar but somehow familiar. "You must shut your fucking mouth. You need to be punished."

With this, the bag over her face was lifted up just enough for a ball-gag to be shoved into her mouth and hastily tied behind her head. The mysterious man pulled the bag back down.

"Kiley," the voice had changed. It became more feminine, and Kiley felt some familiarity with it again. She tried to speak, to call out for Mistress Eva, but she was unable to do much more than grunt into the gag.

She felt a hand around her pants button, unbuttoning them, unzipping them, and for whatever reasoning, she willfully Kiley lifted her legs for them to be removed, panties and all. A set of lips brushed against her warming pussy, an audible sniff, a lip dragging across her pussy lips again, and a sigh of intoxication from her captor. Kiley bucked her groins toward the stranger. In response, the stranger slapped a hand hard against her pubic area, and Kiley grunted out in desire and pain.

There was no doubt now. This was the doing of her Mistress. She felt a cold bit of steel against her neck. "Stay still, honey," the voice called out. "This could hurt."

The steel brushed down her exposed skin, slid just under the neck of her shirt, and within a moment she could hear it slice through the entire length of her shirt and bra, exposing her breasts. The cold steel rested a moment on each nipple, soon followed by a sharp bite for each. Kiley's pussy oozed with desire as two clamps set themselves onto her nipples. Still blinded by the bag over her face, unable to move her arms due to the cuffs, and gagged so she couldn't speak, Kiley was left with no control. Wanting nothing more than to get fucked, she gyrated her hips, begging for it.

"By now you realize what is going on. Or if you don't, you're really sluttier than I thought," Mistress Eva said aloud, no longer a mystery, but still in complete control. "I'm going to take off the mask and show you what I brought you here for."

As the mask came off, Kiley saw that the Mistress was topless, wearing only a pair of leather panties. Her D-cup breasts were gorgeous, perfectly perky, and milky in tone. Her body was fit and just the right amount of curvy for grabbing. Beneath the panties was a noticeable bulge. Perhaps this bulge had always been there and Kiley had just never noticed it, but it brought to her a sense of want she couldn't deny.

"Come," Mistress Eva motioned to her young man, standing off to the side. "You are familiar with Kenneth. He is going to assist us today. Boy, get the rod." He obliged, handing it over to the mistress. The rod was a long stick, rounded on the end with a small metal bit at the very tip. It became obvious that the mistress was intending to fuck her new slave with it.

Kiley once again bucked her hips, desperate for some type of attention and something other than added suspense and teasing. The mistress laughed. "You want this?"

Kiley pleaded into her gag, and the mistress finally obliged, pushing the rod up against Kiley's exposed cunt, spreading the lips just a bit, as if to get a look around them. She rubbed the rod's tip against Kiley's clit, and as juices began to drip from her cunt, the mistress very briefly rubbed the bulge in her panties. The rod slid into her, it's girth enough to make her shiver after the long wait, and the mistress' motions and digging toward her g-spot pushing her toward an orgasm faster than believable. As it began to vibrate, she clenched her fists tight and bucked herself hard against the long skinny rod, pushing herself down on it.

At the very first sight of Kiley's contracting and trembling, a terrible shock rang through the rod and into Kiley, causing her to flail wildly with pain. The gushing from her pussy was so intense that it literally spilled out of her, still convulsing with the electric charge that sent her orgasm spiraling out of control.

When the electricity finally stopped, when the mistress finally stopped shocking her with the rod, Kiley fell flat to the mattress and wept, her cunt still oozing as the rod continued to move inside her, rubbing her as if consoling the violence she'd just experienced.

"You can say no," the mistress said. "Just shake your head if you want to stop."

Kiley didn't shake her head, but instead pushed herself back onto the now stopped rod. Without first realizing it, she had been uncuffed by Kenneth, the mistress' young man, who stood nearby her now with his dick clearly hard in his jeans. She wanted to reach out for it. She wanted to rip it from his jeans and feel his jizz running down her face... and as she did move that hand toward him, the shocking began again. The convulsions caused her to jerk hard, to fling the cunt spittle around the room. It stopped quicker this time.

"No," Mistress Eva demanded. "Get on all fours."

Kiley obliged, discarding the cut up blouse and bra on the ground, and lifting her ass high in the air. The rod rubbed a few times over her dripping slit, pushing hard against the clit, and dipped in once more to wet the tip. It moved across the length of her pussy and to her asshole, where it prodded gently until the hole opened up for it. Once opened, her ass swallowed the tip of the rod, and the sensation of the curved end poking around left her feeling lightheaded. Once more, she was shocked, but only lightly this time before the rod was removed.

A tube entered her butthole. She knew what this meant, and lifted her ass even higher in the air than before. A little bit of the solution leaked into her ass as Kenneth stood to her side. The rod continued to prod around her pussy in the meantime.

As the fluid completely filled her colon, Kiley felt warm, uncomfortable, and completely violated in a way that made her excited. The probing rod let out the tiniest shock, and unable to keep her asshole in control, Kiley felt a bit of the fluid run down her ass cheeks and legs. To her great relief, it hadn't been that long since she'd been completely flushed. Kenneth removed the tube and stepped back to watch.

Once again, Kiley was shocked from within her pussy, this time a long, hard shock that sent her out of control once more. As her body flailed around and flopped, and finally collapsed, the fluids from her asshole spilled out all over the mattress, the floor, the room. And once more, she wept with the pain and humiliation.

Returning with a hose, Kenneth unapologetically began to spray Kiley down, the rod now gone from her, the floor drain taking care of the mess brilliantly, and the medical mattress as clean as ever. Kiley, clean and wet on the bed, now facing the mistress, still had tears running down her face as the cold of the concrete walls and floors made itself known to her.

The mistress stepped forward and climbed between Kiley's legs on the mattress. Shoving them high in the air, the mistress pressed her bulge against Kiley's asshole for just a moment before backing up, lifting one leg, and then the other, and tossing the panties to the side. Her member was adequately sized, unlike her huge breasts. Without any further warning, she jammed her dick straight into Kiley's asshole, pumped hard and fast into her without saying anything at all. Her thumb got a quick suck in her mouth, and she pushed it deep inside of Kiley's cunt as she continued to plow her.

Kiley moaned and grunted into the ball gag, trying not to close her eyes, trying to grasp that her mistress was indeed a transsexual with an enema fetish. All of a sudden, Kiley felt added weight. Looking directly ahead she saw that Kenneth had mounted behind Mistress Eva and was now pushing his dick into her asshole at the same time. Kenneth set the pace, pushing Eva into Kiley with every thrust as Eva continued to finger Kiley's pussy.

As Kenneth reached orgasm, he slammed down hard into the two women, forcing Eva's cock deep inside of Kiley's asshole, Kiley pushing back, enjoying the pressure, screaming through the gag for Eva to cum inside of her. And, as if clockwork, Kenneth lost his load at the same moment that Eva deposited her warm, milky juice deep inside of Kiley's asshole. Almost immediately, Kenneth dismounted, and with Eva's dick still deep inside Kiley, Kenneth licked his Mistress' asshole, tonguing it first before sucking hard to pull out his own jizz, which he greedily swallowed. As he moved away from this, Eva dismounted Kiley and slapped her across the face for seemingly no reason.

As the jizz oozed out of Kiley's butthole, Kenneth took Eva's spot and rubbed his dick over her holes to collect the jizz before pushing it down into Kiley's sopping wet pussy. Still hard and within her cunt, he rolled Kiley over onto her side and continued to pump into her, the orgasm nearing. Just as she neared her release, the familiar feeling of the rod found its way into her loosened asshole, went in deep a few times, and then she shivered... convulsed, both her and Kenneth getting a hard shock. Kenneth exploded once more, deep inside her snatch, and Kiley's body contorted with screams of pain and pleasure as she collapsed, completely exhausted, juices mingling with Kenneth's and spilling out on the mattress.

"Clean her, escort her out," Mistress Eva said coldly, walking out of the room.

Kiley and Kenneth lay there, both weeping, while Kenneth reached behind her head and unhooked the ball gag. Kiley let out a sigh of relief, but didn't say anything, just cuddled closer to Kenneth, forcing his half-flaccid dick to go just a little deeper inside of her.

## #4: Two Women, One Man Group Sex and an Enema Ass Fucking for the Slave Boy

Kiley buried her face into Veronica's wet pussy, lapping up her juices as if she were dying of dehydration in a desert. Veronica pushed down on her head, bucking herself into Kiley's face harder and harder. As she began to shake with an orgasm, Kiley jammed two fingers deep inside her slit, and the contractions swallowed them with a tight pressure that made Kiley want more. As the excitement of the orgasm subsided, Veronica rolled Kiley over, spread her legs, and pushed their privates together. Rubbing their clits against one another, the humped until both came several times. They would have continued, but the alarm clock finally went off, signaling that Kiley needed to get up, ready for work, and make the rounds through the mundanity of office bitch life.

"You could call in," Veronica said, groping Kiley's tit as they lay for a moment in the nude, fighting off the urge to continue and abandon all responsibility.

"You could meet me for lunch," Kiley kissed her neck.

Veronica laughed, "You mean like a couple?"

Kiley blushed, became reserved, and worked her way

out from under the covers. "You don't have to. I was…"

Pulling herself up to Kiley, Veronica pushed herself hard against her new friend. "I'd love to have lunch with you, Kiley." The kissed a few times. "Go on, get ready for work."

###

Sitting at her desk, Kiley brightened up as Veronica came through the door and began talking to Kiley. "I just need a couple more minutes, and I'll be ready to go. There's this great spot just around the block."

Devon, Kiley's co-worker whose sexual advances were mostly mild but consistent, approached the desk. "Who is your gorgeous friend?" he asked.

"Veronica, this is Devon. Devon, Veronica," Kiley mumbled out. They briefly shook hands.

"Are you the girl that stayed the night with Kiley?" Devon laughed at his question, but Veronica leaned in close to him.

"Yes, I am. She ate me out three times this morning," Veronica whispered. Instantly, Devon felt his dick lurch in his pants, his face become red, and a huge smile creep up on his face.

"Never mind him; he fancies he can please several women at any given moment," Kiley laughed, setting her desk's phone to transfer to the relief's cubical and collecting her things. "Let's go."

"Where are you headed?" Devon asked, fishing for an invite.

"We're going to do lesbian things," Kiley patted him on the back.

"It's okay, you can invite him to lunch too," Veronica giggled.

"Fine, do you want to go to lunch with us and ask inappropriate questions?"

"Of course I do."

###

By the end of lunch, Veronica and Devon have made friends. Devon's overtly sexual jokes and inclinations seemed to be a fairly even match with Veronica's appetites for the same. To Kiley's great surprise, she actually enjoyed their exchanges. Still, she worried that Devon might learn too much about her... too much about this new secret life she's leading where nightly sex parties full of enemas, group sex, double penetration…

"We better be getting back," Kiley interrupted them. "I can't really be late, have to man the front desk and let the other girl go to lunch too…" They obliged her.

Driving back to the office, Veronica offered a suggestion. "Maybe the three of us should get together after work sometime?"

Kiley looked over at Veronica with a pleading glare, hoping she wasn't trying to rope him into a night at "The Enema Lounge" where she'd been violated and on show for all to see just a few nights ago.

"Just the three of us," Veronica gave a knowing look, still pleading her case. "See if you can really handle two women at once."

"What are you ladies doing tonight?"

###

Kiley felt unsure about Devon and Veronica coming to her place directly after work, but as Veronica came and picked her up, there was Devon waiting by his car and talking to her again. Swallowing hard, Kiley got in with Veronica and told Devon to follow.

Once back at her place, Veronica took it upon herself to keep things moving along. She knew that Devon was not as talented or confident as he suggested, and she could feel Kiley's uneasiness about the events she'd been forced into. "Let's just go straight to the bed," she said. "No sense trying to pretend we're doing anything else here, right?"

Kiley obliged, Devon following closely behind them, his dick already hard in his pants. Kiley and Veronica began kissing and groping one another, groping each other, and Veronica pulled off her shirt and pants in no time, exposing that she was wearing neither panty nor bra, her supple tits perky and inviting for Kiley's mouth and hand, her cunt already wet and Kiley's finger already plunged inside of her.

Devon stood as if dumbfounded. He stroked himself softly over his pants, and just watched as Veronica tore off Kiley's blouse, popped off her bra, and slid the jeans and panties off her ample ass. Pushing Kiley to the bed, Veronica jumped between her legs playfully and gave Kiley a minute of tonguing and biting to help her relax.

Kiley reached out her hand toward Devon, "Take off those pants already." He obliged quickly, dropping

44

his pants and boxers and moving close to the side of the bed where Kiley laid. As Veronica continued to munch her carpet, Kiley took Devon's rock-hard 7" cock into her hand and began to stroke him before leaning over and giving the tip a long hard suck. As she bobbed on his cock and Veronica dug deep into her pussy with her fingers, Devon couldn't believe his luck.

Bringing her head up from Kiley's cunt, Veronica looked ravenous, covered in juices. "Let's get some dick in her already!"

Devon swapped places with Veronica, repositioning himself between Kiley's legs and pushing the head of his dick across her clit as Veronica watched intently. She groped his balls at the same moment he finally pushed his member into Kiley's sopping wet hole, sending a shiver down his spine. As he began pump-ing, Kiley bucked into him as Veronica swung her leg over Kiley's face and let Kiley's tongue flick her bean, caress her pussy legs, dig deep into her hole.

Devon gave it a solid effort, but Veronica could see by the look on his face that he was having a hard time not jizzing. Her ass still in Kiley's face, she leaned down and found what little space should could to reach Kiley's clit with her tongue as Devon kept pumping into her. Kiley's bucking increased and within a minute she was thrashing about, her juices coating Devon's cock and bringing him close to finishing.

"Nope," Veronica said, slapping Devon across the face, taking him completely by surprise and therefore stopping his orgasm. "I don't know how much stamina you have, but you still have other holes to fill."

While this stopped his immediate release, his excitement only grew with this statement. Pulling out of Kiley, he gave her clit a quick suck, the overstimulation just following her orgasm giving her a good shake, and he proceeded to lay down on the bed next to her. Veronica positioned herself over his cock, still wet from Kiley's cunt, and rubbed her asshole against it. As his pre-cum leaked out, she wetted her ass. To help, Kiley positioned herself to spit on his dick, spit on her asshole, rub it into her asshole, and even shoved a finger into her tight little bum. Pushing herself down on his cock, her sphincter swallowed him completely in one fell swoop. Both Veronica and Devon let out a sigh. Facing him, Veronica pumped up and down a few times on his cock, her tight hole almost more than he could bear. Sitting all the way down on him, she spun around so he could see her back side. This maneuver turned his world upside down.

"I'm... gonna..." he began...

Kiley slapped him hard across the face. "You can come when we're done with you."

Shocked that his mild mannered co-worker was as aggressive as her friend, he withheld a bit longer. Kiley assumed a position to eat Veronica's cunt as she remained seated with his cock deep in her asshole. Only bouncing to the rhythm of Kiley's cunnilingus, Veronica could feel the hard dick pulsating within her, and Devon's hand reaching forward to grope at her titties and look around her to see the action taking place. As she began nearing her orgasm, Veronica pushed Kiley's face into her fuck hole harder, thrashing wildly, bucking against the cock in her ass now, and screaming out. Even before the orgasm had completely ended, Devon, finally taking some initiative on his own, flipped her over and began pounding inside her asshole, a finger finding its way inside her cunt as he continued to fight the urge to blow his load.

"You can come," Kiley said. And come he did. Letting out a curdling yawp, he pushed hard into Veronica's butthole, spurt after spurt of his spunk depositing itself deep inside of her. As he pulled away, half dazed, Kiley pushed him down and swallowed the whole of his dick into her throat, tasting Veronica's asshole, slurping up the jizz leftover on his wang before forcefully kissing him. Diverting her attention to Veronica, she plunged a finger in her ass and encourage the cream pie to leak out, putting her face below it to catch it before sucking on her asshole to get the last bits. Devon watched in amazement as the two women kissed with his asshole-deposited cum swishing between their mouths.

"That was fucking amazing," he said.

As the moment died down, Veronica gave Devon a kiss on the cheek, and Kiley followed. "You actually did a lot better than I'd have thought," Kiley smiled.

"That was fucking amazing," Devon stammered. "I never realized you…"

"Shut up," Kiley said.

"We're gonna have to leave soon…" Veronica pointed out the time. "You were wonderful, Devon, but it's time to say goodbye."

###

That evening, Kiley and Veronica made their way through the supermarket, into the warehouse area, and into the backroom where "The Enema Lounge" events took place. Tonight's showing was small, only three men and two women were present. Kenneth, Mistress Eva's young boy, sat on the couch completely naked except for what appeared to be a cage around his cock and shackles hooking him to the floor.

"Not a lot of people show up for these ones," Veronica whispered to Kiley. "They're not as much about participation, but you should really see it anyway."

"What's going on?" Kiley asked, taking a seat near a couple that had already started fondling each other.

"Just watch…"

A few minutes later, Mistress Eva came out, completely naked, her tranny dick on display, rock hard with a cock ring keeping it overly engorged.

Veronica watched Kiley's face as the Mistress came into the room… realizing there was no surprise, she slapped Kiley on the shoulder playfully. "You knew about the dick already?"

"Of course," Kiley smiled. "Who doesn't?"

"My beautiful little sluts," Mistress Eva addressed the small crowd. "Tonight is one of our special shows. Please remain seated for the duration. I demand that you restrain yourselves from participating and just enjoy the show, go home, and finish whatever sick desires you have then."

The couple fondling each other stopped, wrapped their hands in one another's and sat, watching intent-ly.

Kenneth, the young man chained on the couch, as-sumed the position of his ass being in the air. Eva rolled over the familiar cart, lifted the enema bag and tube, and plunged it into his asshole. His balls and dick still locked away in a small cage, it could be seen lurching and growing and pushing against the con-fines. He looked uncomfortable already. As the fluid filled him up, he looked even more uncomfortable.

With his asshole full of liquid, the tube removed, Mis-tress Eva slapped him hard across the ass. He jerked, but only slightly. She slapped him again. The couple beside Kiley petted each other once more, avoiding private parts and trying not to get in trouble.

Eva removed a paddle from the cart. She slapped it hard against Kenneth's ass, a small spurt of the fluid coming out before he could concentrate on clenching his cheeks tight once more. She slapped him again, but nothing spilled. Eva's dick was still hard and out in the open for all to see. The paddle no longer working, she moved on to a whip, whipping his ass, his back, the soft spots on the back of his legs. Nothing came out of his asshole. He clenched tightly despite the blood red marks forming on his body.

She pulled a few needles from the cart, and moving toward him, she immediately jabbed one into his nipple, and then another. He squeaked in pain and a little tiny bit of fluid came out of his asshole once more. She stroked her dick a few times and pushed it against his face. He willingly opened his mouth for her member, sucking on it long and hard for thirty seconds before she stuck another need into one of his nipples. He bit down on her dick ever-so-slightly, he guard down, a gush of fluid rushing from his asshole.

Her dick wet, she moved to his backside, mounted up near his ass, and without warning pushed into the already full asshole with a brutal force. The fluids from the enema came spilling out all around her cock, down his cock and balls, all over the couch, and all over the floor.

The couple beside Kiley could barely contain themselves. The woman rubbed hard against her man's cock, and Kiley felt a strange and uncomfortable energy about the room that she wasn't sure she enjoyed as a spectator… but knew she enjoyed as a participant.

As Mistress Eva continued to pound her ladydick into her younger slave man, the fluid finally stopped pushing. His dick could be straining against the bars of the cock cage, and his grunts grew louder. To everyone's surprise, his cock all of a sudden shot load after load onto the couch. Not once had it been touched, fondled, even acknowledged... all it took was Eva's enema ass fucking...

The couple beside Kiley squirmed, and now both of them had their hands down each other's pants. Veronica leaned close to Kiley and whispered, "You'll get to see the full show thanks to the couple beside us."

Mistress Eva had not addressed or even remotely acknowledged the small crowd the entire time. So when she shot her glare over towards the couple beside Kiley, they froze up with fear almost instantly. "Come, sit on the floor here," she said to them.

Hesitantly they removed their hands from each other's pants, made their way to the floor, still covered in the clear saline that rushed out of Kenneth's ass as it got plungered by his Mistress. In the filth, the Mistress pumped a few more times, and she pulled out, a bit of the solution spraying and splashing over the couple, and she let out her huge load across the two of them. The shear amount of cum was absurd. It looked like gallons, like there was more fluid from her firehose than the enema bag.

Covered in filth, she instructed both of them to remove their clothes, and they did so eagerly. Kenneth was laid out on the couch, and she had them both lean across his sweaty body as she paddled both of them hard and long. The man's cock dripped with pre-cum, and the woman's cunt left a puddle making its way down her leg. Their flesh red from their paddling, the Mistress pushed her dick up against the woman's cunt to wet herself, and moved on to the man, rubbing her dick across his asshole. She teased them both back and forth for a few minutes, and then left them and walked away from the scene.

A moment later, she returned with a bucket of ice and dumped it over them and Kenneth. The unexpected sensation sobered up the moment, and she followed it with a cold hosing down with a garden hose attached to the sink across the room. Unsatisfied and teased, the couple stood up and thanked their Mistress for correcting their behavior.

Kiley turned to Veronica, "Let's go home now."

## #5: Devon Gets Initiated with an Enema, Needle Play, Anal Sex with the Tranny Mistress, and a Four-person Gangbang Train



When Kiley walked into work, there was Devon. The day before, Devon was surprised when Kiley and Veronica had invited him into a threesome with them. Having worked with Kiley for so long, and made advances to no avail, he never realized just how nasty she could be.

"Kiley!" he said ecstatically as she sat down at her desk. They were both early, and only a few people were in the office. Still, he leaned in close to whisper, "I've been thinking about yesterday."

Kiley barely acknowledged him, "Yeah?"

"That was something else," he continued. "I was hoping it could happen again?"

Kiley looked up at him briefly, taking things out of her bag and setting them up on her desk. "Maybe?" She shrugged at him.

"Is something wrong? Did you not have fun?"

"Devon," Kiley finally gave him some attention. "You

don't want to get mixed in with all the weird shit I've… well you just don't want to do it. Yesterday was awesome. Maybe it'll happen again, but you really should know when to stay away from trouble."

At this, Devon felt his dick start to grow in his pants, walked around the desk, and kneeled down to be closer to Kiley's level where she sat. "That's where you're wrong," he said confidently. "I most definitely want to be involved with all the weird shit you have been doing."

Kiley laughed. "I'll think about it and let you know at the end of the day."

###

At lunch, Kiley met with Veronica, who had been spending almost all of her free time with Kiley while indulging in the unsavory sex acts at "The Enema Longue." Discussing Devon's insistent behavior, Veronica couldn't help but laugh.

"We could give him a test run," she said.

Kiley looked at her hard, "A test run? What? I have to work with this dude every day."

"A test run… we'll, you know, do some of the freaky

shit to him ourselves before inviting him to the longue."

Kiley thought back to how she'd learned about "The Enema Longue." It was really by chance. An older gentlemen was talking with his wife about the events that happened there, and Kiley eavesdropped until they made it clear they knew she was listening. They gave her the information she needed to contact Kenneth, Mistress Eva's boy toy, and the rest was history. Now here was Veronica, perhaps the world's sweetest cum slut, who had inadvertently become Kiley's...

"Fine," Kiley said. "I'll invite him..."

Kiley felt distracted. For the first time, she was wondering just what Veronica was doing with her all this time. They weren't remotely exclusive, but it felt like a relationship was forming still. As Kiley stared into her salad, Veronica nudged her.

"If you're that worried about it, just tell him to fuck off," she said, stroking Kiley's hair.

Kiley shook her head. "It's not that. It's just... why are you spending so much time with me?"

Veronica blushed. Kiley had never seen this happen before, and the strange sway of Veronica's head told her that something real must be there. "Look, I don't know what it is yet. It's still new," Veronica answered. "Is it enough to say I like being around you?"

Kiley kissed Veronica hard on the mouth. An elderly couple saw this and shook their heads.

###

At the end of her shift, Kiley sat at her desk awaiting Devon to make his way out for the day. As he approached, she smiled at him. "Okay," she said.

"Okay?" he asked.

"Okay… as in come over to my place. But you have to promise to keep all my weird shit to yourself."

Without another word, the two of them left for the day, made their way to Kiley's place, and found Veronica waiting inside. Veronica had cleared off the dining room table and set up a massage bed. Kiley had no idea where she found the time to procure these things, but she was glad that she'd thought of an easy way to keep the mess at a minimal. Veronica was buck naked already. Her perky tits were erect, and her landing strip instantly caught Devon's attention.

"Hello," Devon said, his dick already at full mast.

"Shut the fuck up," Veronica barked, taking the lead. "Get your fucking clothes off."

Devon obliged, stripping down and approaching Veronica. Kiley approached Veronica as well, bumping Devon out of the way before she fondled her breasts a little and gave her a long, slow kiss. She reached her hand to Veronica's honey hole to dip her fingers in and get a taste. Devon went to stroke himself when Veronica pulled away from Kiley and slapped him hard across the face.

Taken aback, Devon took a couple steps away from the women, but held his ground, trying his best not to tear up. "Get on the table, on your stomach."

"Is there a safe word?" Devon asked.

Kiley, feeling a little unsure of her role, chimed in, "Are you such a pussy that you need a safe word? Seriously, I let you into my secret life, and you're asking about a fucking safe word?"

Devon looked at her in disbelief. "Of course not… I can handle anything…"

"Promise. Right now. Promise you will obey everything we tell you to do," Kiley grabbed his balls and squeezed hard. "You begged for this, now promise you'll do as you're told no matter what happens next."

Devon felt himself sweating, but as Kiley's grip on his balls increased, he felt his dick grow harder. He nodded in agreement, "Anything. I promise." Kiley released his balls slightly before giving them a hard, painful tug. He let out a gasp. "On the fucking table then."

Devon climbed on the massage table and lay down on his stomach. "Stay put," Veronica say.

Veronica kissed Kiley once more. "That was… that… I need to eat your fucking pussy." Veronica yanked at Kiley's pants, pulling them and her panties off almost instantly before pushing her onto a nearby chair and burying herself into Kiley's pussy. Devon watched, pushing his dick slightly against the padded massage table as Veronica continued to munch on Kiley's cunt.

As Kiley reached her orgasm, Veronica buried her nose into her slit even further, lapped at her juices, and slurped down whatever she could. Devon lay there in complete ignorant bliss, still pumping his hips into the table a bit.

As Veronica pulled away from Kiley, she made her way to the kitchen table and lifted up one of the towels to reveal a paddle. Immediately she grabbed it and slapped Devon's ass as hard as she possibly could, immediately making it red, and sending a shooting pain through his body.

"FUCK!" he screamed out.

"Did I tell you to dry hump my table?" Veronica said. "Face down, ass up."

Devon obliged, watching as Kiley joined Veronica behind him. Kiley reached out and tugged on his dick a couple times, watching the pre-cum drip down.

"This is pretty exciting," Kiley said to Veronica, taking the paddle from her and slapping Devon hard against the ass once more. Upon contact he fell back to his original position, but quickly recovered and lifted his ass in the air.

"Is this what you wanted?" Kiley asked him. "Is it what you expected?" She spit on his asshole, holding his cock once more but not stroking it, only applying more and more pressure. Veronica returned to the table, lifting the towels to find a small butt plug. She sucked on the plug for a second and rubbed it against his asshole.

"I..." Devon started. "I didn't..."

"You are a pussy, huh? Didn't you just promise?" Kiley scolded him. "This is your last chance. You can leave now and never talk of any of this to me again, or..."

"I promise, I promise," he assured her.

Veronica shoved the plug completely into his ass, a new sensation for him, and Kiley let go of his dick. As Veronica pumped the small plug in and out of him, an audible popping sound each time, Kiley made her way back to the table to take a look at what else Veronica had procured. To her surprise, there wasn't much else besides a few more dildos and plugs, some nipple clamps, and a set of needles.

"Clamps," Veronica suggested. Kiley smiled, taking the nipple clamps and without warning clamping them down on Devon's exposed man nips. He struggled in pain but didn't fight it. Veronica replaced the small plug with a dildo, slightly larger, and continued to pump it into his asshole. His dick was still rock hard, and the new sensations were still not enough to drive him away.

Veronica looked at the clock and then at Kiley. "I have a surprise for you..."

Suddenly, the front door opened. In came Kenneth and Mistress Eva, the two mainstays at "The Enema Longue." In her hand she held an enema.

"Who's that?" Devon called out, trying to crane his neck. Kiley grabbed the paddle, and she paddled him on the ass once more. "Stay still, you little bitch." She surprised herself with her aggression.

"Mistress," Veronica acknowledged Eva. "Here he is. Just for you."

Kenneth readied the enema, slipping the dildo out of Devon's ass and working the hose into him slowly. "This is going to feel warm and you may feel full. Try to keep your ass up high."

"Wait..."

Before Devon could say anymore, Kenneth began to fill Devon's asshole with the solution. "Clench tight please." Once full, Kenneth stepped away and greeted Kiley with a kiss on the cheek. His dick was hard in his pants and Kiley grabbed at it, remembering how large it was and how full it made her asshole feel.

Mistress Eva addressed the room. "Ladies, and slutty

little boys, I can't thank you enough for thinking of me for tonight's event. I know you're probably freaking out a little bit on that table," she laughed. "You will experience new things tonight, and perhaps you'll experience more after tonight. You are special. You are blessed. You, a man with three mistresses, are no longer your own man. That is something to be truly thankful for."

With this, Mistress Eva grabbed his cock and began to stroke him. He clenched hard as she licked his ball sack, trying not to spill anything. She sucked on the tip of his head, and then she released him completely to approach him from the front. Suddenly, he looked up and at the same instant her dick was sliding across his face. He thought about fighting it. He thought about letting the fluid spill from his ass and taking off into the night completely naked, covered in the filth. Instead, he opened his mouth and took her dick between his lips.

Veronica, Kiley, and Kenneth all clapped at this breakthrough. Kenneth took off his clothes, and rubbed his dick against Kiley's behind and between her legs as Veronica moved back to the table full of goodies. She took out the package of needles and sterilized them with a lighter. As Kiley mounted Kenneth's dick on a nearby chair, Veronica jammed one of the needles through his nipple. He let out a mellow yelp and kept bucking against Kiley's gushing cunt.

Moving away from his mouth, Mistress Eva once again went to the back side of Devon, whose ass was about to explode. Veronica approached him as well, needles in hand. As a needle slid into what nipple skin was exposed within the confines of the clamps, he lost control and a bit of the fluid shot out from his asshole. At the moment of a second needle going into the other nipple, Mistress Eva had jumped on the table, took her ample dick, and shoved it deep into his ass, the fluids shooting out as he collapsed with the pain of the needle, the intrusion of a tranny's dick. The secretion covered Mistress Eva's cock, legs, balls, and he collapsed onto the table once more, Eva now forcing him to lay on his side, his dick still rock hard as she pounded into his asshole.

Kiley rode hard on Kenneth's dick, watching the entire scene. As Kenneth felt himself nearing completion, he motioned for her to get off, and he positioned himself in front of Devon, unleashing a huge load all over Devon's stomach, dick, balls, and even his face. Devon licked at it without moving, unsure if he was in heaven or hell.

As Mistress Eva continued to plow into him, Veronica took his slippery jizz-covered dick and began to lick it clean, lick the balls clean, and suck on his cock for a moment or two before backing herself up against it and sliding it against her asshole, lubing herself up before pushing hard against his dick and feeling the fullness as Eva continued to push and pull him from within. Devon began to rock into Veronica's ass as well.

Kiley stroked Kenneth's cock a few times, just to make sure it was hard. "Fuck her too," she said, totally engrossed in the show before her and her powerful role in it. Obliging her demand, Kenneth joined the three fucking, shoving his dick into Veronica's sopping wet cunt and pumping into her slowly.

Mistress Eva continued to pump into Devon's asshole, still covered in the emissions from the enema. Devon continued to push into Veronica's asshole, and Kenneth pushed hard into Veronica's cunt, increasing his speed. It wasn't long before everyone began to have an orgasm. As if they were one entity, the chain started with Mistress Eva blasting her warm jizz into Devon's virgin asshole. The warmth of it, the added slipperiness, and the taboo of the entire evening sent him over the edge, and he unleashed gobs of jizz deep inside of Veronica's asshole. Kenneth, who was trained at this type of thing, took his cue and unleashed another load inside her sloppy wet cunt. The pile soon pulled apart, and there was Kiley, pushing Veronica to the other side of the table, lapping up the jizz from her asshole, from her cunt, and then burying her face deep within the folds of her pussy. Within moments, Veronica let out a loud scream, shaking violently, and Kiley dug in once more, her face squished between Veronica's legs during her intense orgasm.

Mistress Eva and Kenneth were already dressed when Kiley lifted her head from the sweet nectar pot. Her face was covered in jizz, and there was a smile there when she saw Devon crying a little bit.

Without excusing themselves, Eva and Kenneth simply left. Devon began making his way to his clothes, thinking it best for him to do the same. Kiley grabbed his arm. "You can stay for a bit. Take a shower… talk if you need to."

"I…" Devon stammered. "I… it's fine, I can just…"

"It's really okay," Kiley stroked his arm.

"I'm just confused," Devon said. "But thank you… I would like to take a shower… if it's okay with both of you."

"Of course," Kiley smiled at him.

He looked at Veronica, and she laughed menacingly.

"Who the fuck said you could leave? Who do you think is gonna clean this mess?"

# Back Room BDSM

## #1: Enema for the Slave

Jennifer had a choker around her neck, attached to a metal chain meant to lead her into whatever perils, lustful joys, or strange new adventurous that Susan may have had in mind for her at the time. The moment they reached the back room of the bar, the door was shut and all sounds of patronage lost.

Susan tied the chain around what looked to be a handrail, and removed a pocket knife from seemingly out of nowhere in her tight dress. Jennifer seemed to moan, the sound muffled by the pair of slobbery panties jammed down her mouth.

"Now, now, I told you not to talk," Susan giggled, placing the knife above Jennifer's chest and very lightly, as not to cut her, sliding it down to where her top met her skin. Slicing off the shirt, and then the bra, she exposed Jennifer's bare chest, the remnants of the clothes hanging off to the sides. Susan then slit the top of Jennifer's skirt, another moan ensued, but Susan proceeded by literally tearing if off of the young woman's delicate body. Her dirty panties were still in her mouth, and her shaven slit was exposed with clear signs of wetness seeping down her legs.

There were marks from their previous sessions still visible. Susan had no problem being aggressive, and while Jennifer seemed to moan and gasp and fight it at times, she willingly came back, always wearing the choker intended for the leash. Scratches, small cuts, and even what appeared to be a small rash, but was actually the result of multiple needles being inserted, were plainly evident.

The room was dark and dingy, but overall it appeared to be kept clean. The items inside did not always make the most sense to Jennifer, but she knew that Susan planned ahead. In some cases, she gave hints to what Jennifer should expect.

"Do you want to know what I have in store for you today?" Susan laughed. "Are you ready to be exposed? To let others know that you're just a worthless shit bucket?" Susan continued her speech, getting closer and whispering lower and lower as she did so. "Would you be opposed to having guests tonight?"

Jennifer wanted to say no to the request, but she knew that she had no reason to. She knew that she would ultimately appreciate everything that Susan did for her. Everything that Susan had come up with was part of a much larger plan, leading to a final moment of humiliation so grand that Jennifer knew she would stop coming back… or be banished. That moment is what she sought. The complete breaking of her soul past the point of just sexuality and humiliation. It is what drove her to continue showing up, continue wearing the collar day and night regardless of who may see it. Nobody had quite asked about it yet, but a few comments had been made. Still, someone out there knew what a slut she was.

"I need you to tell me," Susan pressed on. Jennifer nodded, but Susan persisted. "I need to hear you say yes."

Jennifer tried to speak through the panties, having not been given permission to discard them from her mouth yet. The taste of her own juices had long since left the panties, and now her mouth felt dry and uncomfortable, but she knew better than to misstep. Susan has warned her time and time again that the first misstep means banishment from her services. From her guidance and love. For what that love was worth, if anything.

Susan seemed to disapprove. "I suppose I will just untie you then."

Jennifer fought harder to get her voice through the panties without them dropping from her mouth. Susan grabbed her by the face, yanked out the panties, and finally Jennifer muttered, "Yes, I would love to meet you guests, mistress."

"Very good," Susan said, peeling down the remnants of her top and bra before throwing them on the ground and walking to the large storage container on the other side of the room. From this tote, she took out a few items that Jennifer couldn't quite see. She could tell there was a bottle or two, but she had no idea what was in them. There were many other items as well, all of which were set on a cart that Susan wheeled over to her. Jennifer could see two sets of shackles, a spray bottle of what appeared to be water, several dildos, and then a few bulges peeking out from under a towel.

"First, we must prepare you." With the leash still tied off, Susan cuffed the shackles on Jennifer's arms and legs. She untied the leash and dragged the shambling Jennifer to a bed in the middle of the room along with the cart.

"Stay on this bed until I allow you to move."

"Yes, mistress." Jennifer lay on her back, looking straight up but still noticing through the corner of her eyes that a large bucket lay next to the bed for some reason.

Without any further warning, Susan unlocks the door, and in walked several people dressed completely in black, head to toe, even their faces covered in was appeared to be spandex. In the darkness of the room it was impossible to tell if they're male or female, human or alien, old or young. All Jennifer knew was that there was a crowd watching her as her twat lay exposed, wet with worry and excitement. There were four of them in total.

Susan moved back to Jennifer, and gestured by physically moving her that Jennifer should move her ass straight in the air.

"You," Susan motioned. "Use that spray bottle to clean off our subject." The first of the guests moved to the cart, picked up a small spray bottle of water, and hosed Jennifer down. Jennifer lapped at the few drops that reached her mouth, finally able to cure the lack of moisture created from the panties.

"You, spit on her ass." Susan demanded another one of the people in complete body suits. The small body made its way to Jennifer, lifted the mask from their face slightly, and spit directly on the butthole.

"You," Susan pointed to another, "pick something from this cart to stretch her out."

Jennifer cringed at the thought, but didn't dare speak in front of the guests. The third guest found a tapered instrument, a dildo supposedly, and used the tip to spread the spit from the second guest, who spit again on the butthole as the second guest slid it in slowly. The tip had no problem going in, but the tightness of Jennifer's sacred eye became apparent as the tapered prosthetic continued to dig into her anus. Jennifer moaned loudly, even more juices flowing from her snatch than before.

"You, now," Susan said, "as I promised, you may do whatever you like."

The final guest, now out of the shadows, was clearly a man. It wasn't a moment later that he stood above Jennifer, within her sight of view, and his hard member waved above her face, still contained in the stretchy material of his full body suit. He gingerly rubbed one of her tits, leaning forward so his member dangled mere inches from her. Then he lifted his mask just enough to allow him to suckle on the other breast's nipple. His breath was measured and faintly sweet to her. He looked as though he wanted to say something, but instead moved to watch the others, one using the taper to stretch her ass, one rubbing her pussy and no longer spitting on her, and the other simply watching as well. When a finger went into Jennifer's snatch, she squirmed and muttered a simple and quiet, "Yes."

"SILENCE!" Susan screamed. Everyone immediately stopped, and backed off of Jennifer, who felt too aroused to contain her desires. "You will not speak a single word. Or make a single sound. Every time you do, I will punish you. You now," Susan directed her attention to one of the masked participants. "Use the whip on her bare ass."

With her ass still in the air, a position that has begun to bring her pain, Jennifer was aware of what is about to happen to her. The masked guest took the whip from the cart, and without any further warning slapped it down on her bare ass as hard as possible, leaving an instant welt. Jennifer cried out in pain, and Susan nodded to do it again.

While the pain was its own type of pleasurable, the attention of all four guests had Jennifer feeling elated, and the sharp feeling of the whip could simply not compare to this on its own. She bit down hard on her lip and suppressed her noises as well as possible, and now in silence, the room seemed to take on a life of its own, the guests now doing what they wanted rather than following direction.

The tapered dildo had sufficiently stretched her ass, and now it moved in and out, bringing along with it the shape of her bottom around the anus as it pulled out. Jennifer bit her lips to hold back her screams of pleasure. She knew that she could not cum either, and in this knowledge, it made it all the harder to fight it off as one of the guests, clearly a woman now, had her face buried just inches from the tapered dildo and directly on her crotch, lapping up the juices from her snatch like she lived for it.

The third guest continued to just watch from the side, while the man had exposed himself and began smacking his dick across Jennifer's face in an almost comical way. Finally, he slapped her directly in the mouth, and Jennifer moaned a bit, wanting to ask her mistress a question, but unable to communicate.

"Open your mouth," Susan confirmed. Within that split second, she had the man's dick down her throat, almost gagging her, using the opportunity to emit noises from her other pleasures.

Susan and the third guest congregated at the cart and began fooling around with the items that had been hidden beneath the towel. Jennifer wanted to divert her attention to their tasks, but being air-tight with a guest at each of her orifices, it became impossible to focus, let alone think or reason. Her vision had already blurred. Her sense of awareness was fading quickly, and all she could focus on was holding back from the orgasm, holding back from the shattering of the moment and the reprimand she might receive if she should explode before given permission. It was not going to be a good reprimand. It wasn't going to be the joy of a whip on her ass. It would be much worse, possibly banishment.

"Just a few minutes," Susan said to the guests.

At this que, the male guest moved the guests from between her legs, taking over the tapered dildo and plunging his dick deep inside her pussy with no warning. The other guests just watched as she was double penetrated.

Jennifer couldn't stop herself from letting out a loud whimper. The warmth of the man's dick deep inside her felt too good, and the pressure had built up too much. She was slippery all over, still wet from being sprayed down. The noise was not lost on Susan.

"Punish her," Susan said to the man. He pulled out of her pussy and repositioned his dick to her asshole, the taper still in about halfway. Jennifer squirmed but didn't resist and he pushed his dick into the hole with the taper. Her asshole felt like it might tear from the girth of the two members, one flesh and one rubber.

But again, like the whip, she enjoyed this type of pain, and had an even harder time not making a sound.

"You may make noises now," Susan said, almost laughing.

Immediately a primal scream came from Jennifer. It was almost frightening just how horrid and angry and sad and distressing it was, but it encouraged the man to push into her harder, the taper and his member both fully lodged within her small sacred eye. Stretched beyond belief, he removed the taper, pushed into her a few more times, and released his seed deep inside her asshole, and again spurted on the outside, rubbing his dick around it as if it needed to be lubricated again.

The fire burning inside Jennifer's loins was too intense for her. The orgasm she kept being denied would never come at this point, would never be granted, and her heart swelled with a fear she didn't understand. Perhaps banishment would be the only solution to reach this orgasm? Perhaps, it would be worth it.

"Did you enjoy getting your ass stretched?" Susan looked over Jennifer. "Now lay on your side."

The man joined the other watching guests, one of them holding what appeared to be an enema bag, already full of water.

"I think before we let you cum, we'll have to let you enjoy a little cleaning. You, again with the hose." One of the guests brought back out the spray bottle and hosed down Jennifer, whose sweat and jizz and wetness all mingled together.

The man and another guest, the woman who had eaten Jennifer's snatch, repositioned themselves in front of Jennifer's face, just a few steps away, and the woman began to clean the man's pole with her mouth.

"You watch them, now," Susan commanded. "If you look away, they'll tell me."

Jennifer forced her eyes open, almost trying not to blink at all as she watched the man's dick covered in her tainted assiness was licked up by the woman guest. His dick sprung back into action as she continued. One of her hands were down her tight all-black pants, and Jennifer wanted nothing more than to join the two of them. Meanwhile, she could hear the others working on something in the background. The large tub was moved to a place behind her, and finally she felt the tip of the enema bag around her sphincter. One of the guests plunged it into her, startling her even though she had some idea of what was going on.

"We are going to fill you up completely," Susan said. "Do not release. Do not take your eyes away from the show, and don't say a word until I say you can."

Jennifer wanted to nod, wanted to show her appreciation for all her mistress was doing for her, and all the guests were offering with their talents. Instead, she watched on as the female guest fingered herself under her pants and came not once, but twice while never missing a beat sucking off the male guest.

As the liquid began to press against her insides, filling her quicker than she had imagined, and sending her into a dizzy and frantic search for release, she watched as the man spurt his seed first on the woman's face before quickly aiming for Jennifer. The feeling of his warm jizz splashing on her as the last of the fluid entered her asshole made her almost blackout. Her eyes rolled, and all her energies were focused on clenching her butt checks together.

"Okay, please be seated," Susan said to the guests. "Your services are done, but you may stay and watch."

The guests all moved to a bench along the wall. They

were out of sight, but Jennifer could hear them rustling amongst each other, even touching one another.

Susan stooped down to look Jennifer in the face, the jizz still sliding down her cheek. "Are you ready to release? You may respond, but stay silent afterwards."

"Yes, mistress," Jennifer mumbled. Susan removed the tube from Jennifer's anus, and returned to her face. Jennifer clenched for dear life, trying to hold everything in until she had actual consent.

"Would you prefer that I whip you a few times first?" Susan asked, not really asking a question, as she stood up, snatched the whip from the cart, and immediately slapped it against Jennifer's ass several times. The pain wasn't an issue, but trying to retain her composure, her stretched sphincter was just unable to contain all the liquid anymore, and a few spurts came out and into the bucket.

"Do you wish to anger me? Do you want to be banished?" Susan scoffed. In almost the same moment, one of the guests could be heard moaning in pleasure.

"No, mistress, I am trying..."

"You know I hate that word," Susan said, smacking

her ass harder this time, leaving several marks across it. Jennifer clenched harder this time and kept in the liquid trying so desperately to escape her.

"Yes, mistress, I am sorry…"

"Never mind. I know how to punish you," Susan said, then facing the guests and saying, "You are all excused. Thank you for your efforts."

The guests left without another word or sound.

"Don't release yourself until after I get back," Susan demanded.

"Mistress…"

"Don't." Susan said, the door clicking behind her without another sound.

## #2: Rewarded with Double Penetration

Jennifer contemplated her situation, clenching her butt checks as hard as possible trying not to purge her bowels from the enema fluid she held in. Mistress Susan would punish her in the worst way should she release before her return. She may even get banished.

Jennifer was uncertain how long she laid there naked, jizz still on her face, and her twat still aching for a final release, her asshole filled to the brim with fluid from the unexpected enema. This was certainly torture, and despite the ache in her loins to have an earth shattering orgasm, she was almost certain she wasn't having fun anymore.

Maybe it was never fun. Maybe she would be left here forever, shackled to the bed in the back room of a bar. Maybe someone unexpected would discover her.

It didn't matter. At this point, she was still resolved to clench and keep quiet until her mistress returned. It was probably only ten minutes but it felt like eternity. Still, Jennifer had never felt so relieved as when Susan finally walked back into the room, Jennifer was almost certain she would be allowed to cum before all this was over, and more importantly, be allowed to release the horrid liquid in her bowels.

"You've done well," Susan said, looking into the bucket and seeing it mostly empty. Susan bent over her and unlatched the shackles around her arms and legs, and said simply, "When I leave again, you may release the fluid inside of you. Clean up after yourself. There are cleaning supplies and an extra set of clothes in the bathroom. If I come back and this place isn't clean, you will be punished."

"Thank you, mistress," Jennifer said sheepishly, still holding the liquid in and awaiting her Mistress to leave.

Susan didn't respond, and only backed out of the room saying one last task, "I will be in contact. Don't touch yourself. Don't let anyone else touch you. Lock the door behind you."

The moment the door clicked, Jennifer unleashed the fluid stored in her rectum, the sound of it rushing into the large metal tub echoed, it was so loud in the silent room. After cleaning herself up, cleaning up the room, and dressing, she slowly poked her head around the door.

It was morning. The bar was closed, and the only person around was a lone bartender that appeared to be cleaning and setting up for the night to come.

"Have a beautiful day," the bartender said to Jennifer with a smile.

Jennifer smiled back. It would be a beautiful day, even if she didn't have much time to get rest before work.

###

Jennifer worked at a Build-A-Bear workshop for several years before finally getting her degree in Communications and getting a job with their HR department. It beat the hell out of working with children, but the workers weren't that much better when it came down to it. Most days were spent filing paper work and working through people's grievances on their paychecks.

Her boss, a handsome man in his forties, was constantly coming on to her. She didn't mind, but knew that he was married and his wife was a young woman as well, that this man was a perpetual womanizer. Still, sitting at work, unsatisfied from the events of the night before, she watched him walk around the office, his large cock visible through his tight pants.

"Jessica," he said approaching her.

"Jennifer…"

"Jennifer, you look preoccupied today. Is there anything I could do to help you?" he continued. "Perhaps you need to take an extended lunch with some company?" He winked at her.

"No, no, I'm fine." Jennifer wanted to fuck his brains out. Who cares if he knew her name? But in the back of her head rang Susan's voice demanding that she not satiate her horniness. The cream pooled in her panties a bit, and she excused herself to the restroom. "I just need to wash my face and get a coffee."

"Offer always stands, Jessica," her boss blocked her path for just a moment, very close to her, his member touching the back of her ass. He turned to face her, and winked again as she walked off. She knew he was corny and a horrible person, but still her juices continued to flow even more and it took all she had not to pleasure herself in the restroom or take him up on his offer. The idea of his large dick deep inside her twat drove her crazy, and the resulting workday was tortuous and involved a lot of cleanup of her cooch juices in the restroom, as not to stain her pants. Still, she refrained.

###

Finally away from work, Jennifer made her way home to finally get some actual rest and hopefully put aside her sexual desires. Tossing her bag and keys on the counter, she made her way directly to the couch and turned on the television. Resting her head, she fell asleep fairly quickly.

Not fifteen minutes later, her phone rang. "Mistress," she said sleepily.

"Come by tonight. I want to reward you for your good behavior today." Without another word, Susan hung up the phone.

Jennifer knew that "tonight" meant 11PM. This gave her a few hours to rest, but her anticipation made it impossible, and the phrase, "good behavior today," made her curious as to what Susan actually knew about her day to day life.

###

Jennifer walked into the establishment a few minutes early, sat down at the bar, and noticed the same bartender that had wished her well that morning.

"Back again, I see. What'll it be; on the house." He smiled.

"Just a shot of tequila," Jennifer smiled back. "I'm meeting someone soon…"

"Coming up."

What did this bartender know about the back room?

No sooner had the bartender sat down the drink did Susan appear behind Jennifer. "Quickly now." Jennifer took the shot back, sucked a lime, waved at the bartender, and then followed Susan as she led the way to the back room.

Opening the door, the room appeared as she had left it that morning. Clean and well maintained, the bed in the center of the room. Sitting on the bed was a man dressed completely in black, as before, spandex covering almost every inch of his body. Unlike before, all the lights were on in the room, and Jennifer's eyes darted immediately to the man's bulging package trapped in the tight spandex pants that made up part of his getup. She supposed secrecy of the other guests was of utmost importance.

"Undress for him. This is your reward for your good behavior today. You've done very well, and you have pleased me. In return, I have brought back one of our guests from last night for you. Does this make you happy?"

"Yes, mistress," Jennifer said shyly. As she undressed, the man in the black body suit stroked himself through his pants, the bulge becoming engorged and pronounced.

Jennifer's breasts were a C cup, supple and perky. Her cunt was clean shaven, already dripping in anticipation, and her asshole still ached from the night before.

"Let him do what he will," Susan said. "I will be watching."

"Mistress," Jennifer wanted to ask a question but stopped herself. "Thank you." She knew that she would be told when she could finally come.

Susan seemed to disappear on the sidelines as the fully naked Jennifer approached the man in black. He didn't say a word, but stood and motioned for her to come closer to him. He brushed his hands, the only part of his body exposed, across her naked body, groping at her tits with a lustful intention, pushing himself against her, his bulge warm against her cold skin in a familiar manner.

Reaching a hand down, he caressed her clitoris and smeared her wetness around it before bringing his hand to his nose to get a smell. She wanted to reach out and grab his throbbing member, but knew that he was in control and she should only obey.

"Ass up on the bed," he said sternly, in a strange and disguised voice. She obliged, lying down on the bed and lifting her ass up while burying her face in the mattress. Her cunt spread open beautifully, strings of her love juices making their way down her legs and marks on her ass cheeks from her punishment the night before.

He knelt down, lifting up his mask just enough to begin softly licking her asshole. He then sucked on her pussy lips one at a time before pushing his tongue deep inside her. She quivered but restrained herself from getting too aroused, from pushing past the threshold of no return, the white milkiness of blissful release she had so longed for.

Without warning, his dick was out and poking around her slit, lubricating the dick she had so desperately wanted. "Do you want a taste?" He asked, again with the strange voice, not allowing her a moment to answer before making his way to her mouth and having her take in his large cock.

It occurred to her that she had heard this man speak before, but she was uncertain that he had spoken the night before, and it was of a great worriment that she realized she may actually know this man. Still, she remained silent, his dick in her mouth for another moment before he pulled away and returned to prodding around her slit, sliding his dick along it lengthwise so the head rubbed on the clit some more as he grasped at her tits and mouthed her bare back with his lips.

She ached for him to slam his dick deep inside her, and when the moment finally came, the warmth and fullness made it impossible for her to hold back a whimper. Her cream oozed out along the sides of his dick as he made a few slow thrusts before jamming her harder than she could have imagined. Still, she held back on that final release.

"You did good today, Jennifer," the man said again, no longer disguising his voice.

Her heart stopped for a moment. A tightness and fear spread into her that made her clench down on his dick and gasp for air. He kept pushing, but at that moment she realized that the man that fucked her now and the man that fucked her last night was indeed her boss. The guy that ran the show in the Build-a-Bear shop was now doing the stuffing. He had known all along.

She gasped again, almost certain she would have a panic attack, faint, die from the pure humiliation of the situation. She was doomed. She was done for. He knew her secret, and he knew she was nothing but a slut. All those times she'd ignored his advances, he knew what she was. He knew he was simply tempting her, and he reported back to Mistress Susan.

In this tense situation, the tightness of her orifice excited her boss, and it was then that he shot his load deep inside her cunt. The warmth of it reminder her that she was a slut, a useless piece of meat to this man, to the mistress. And in that, she found some comfort. It didn't matter.

As he pulled out, he said, "Roll over, I want to watch it come out."

She moved onto her back and onto the edge of the bed. The man fingered her pussy just enough for his jizz to start dripping out, intermingled with the insane amount of fluid from her own orifice. She looked up at him, and he removed his mask.

"Now you know," he said. "But don't worry. It is a secret we share."

Susan had sat watching the entire thing, listening to the exchange, and watching the horror on Jennifer's face as she discovered the truth. Recovering from the shock, Jennifer wanted to beg to be allowed to cum, but instead just wiped the man's jizz from her coochie and tasted it for both of them to see.

"You have really been such a good little slut today," Susan said, now approaching them with a strap-on already attached. "Lift her up."

Jennifer's boss did as commanded, picking up Jennifer and hoisting her naked body against his chest. His member had not lost its rigidity, and she could feel it once again sliding against the slick of their intermingled juices around her cunt. Sliding her down, he settled his dick inside her, pumping with shallow thrusts. By now, her juices had covered her asshole, and she could feel the tip of the strap on Susan wore penetrating the puckered hole, still not completely healed from the night before. As it slid into her, she felt fuller than she had ever before, even fuller than with the enema. Slowly, the two of them pumped into her over and over, in and out, in a rhythm so delicate and measured it almost lulled Jennifer into a sleep-state, a daze that left her incapable of understanding everything going on in the room, her small body still in the air, supported by man and dick and strap-on.

The daze continued as they laid her down on her side and continued in each of her holes. Unable to react at all, she lay almost lifeless, only her juices seeping and seeping and seeping until a large puddle had destroyed the sheets and made its way onto the ground below them. They began thrusting much harder, her ass and pussy being pulled in one direction and then pushed in the other. When she took in a sharp breath, Susan whispered, "Come now, you may release."

One thrust from each of them later, and Jennifer could no longer see. Her vision went white. Her body convulsed violently, and she began to cry out horrible shrieks while tears ran down her face. Her boss exploded in her once more, and Susan pushed into her as deep as possible. As her juices squirted out from the sides of the man's dick, she continued to cry out loud, unintelligible noises that were the room not sound proof might scare the patrons in the bar.

When the moment was finally over, Susan and the man slid out of her holes, the man slapping his wang across her ass a few times to get the last few drops out of his member.

"You may be excused," Susan said to him.

"See you tomorrow, Jennifer," he winked, even though she couldn't see him. He left the room without another sound, pulling his pants up as he did, presumably going to another room to change before leaving entirely.

Jennifer laid there naked, covered in sweat, her juices completely soaking the area around her, and jizz still flowing out of her cunt.

"You've been good, and I have rewarded you, but don't expect to always be rewarded. I know you're a dirty slut, and I know you're usually a bad, bad girl."

"Yes, mistress," Jennifer managed to whimper.

Susan removed the strap on and threw it on the bed next to the still crying, shaking girl. "Now clean up after your fucking self."

## #3: Four Guests Punish the Slave

Jennifer wasn't sure why, but she hadn't heard from Mistress Susan in almost a week since being "rewarded" for her good behavior. During this time she had restrained herself from masturbating and jumping the bones of the men that worked with her at the Build-a-Bear Workshop. Even her boss, who she knew now was one of Mistress Susan's special guests and had penetrated all of Jennifer's holes just a week ago, was off limits for her. He hadn't mentioned anything about their sordid encounters in the back room dungeon that Susan kept for her clients and submissives. Every day, she stared hard at his cock in his well fitted pants, and dreamed of once again being skewered on his pole. His professionalism seemed almost too forced, though, and the lack of attention he was giving her was out of the normal. It's as if the Mistress forbid him to continue his flirtatious and suggestive attitude towards Jennifer. She almost followed her urges to make a move toward him, but she knew very well that he would report back to Susan. And of course, she knew better than to go to the bar and look for Susan. That wouldn't do.

To distract herself from the lack of physical action, humiliation, and bondage, she attempted to take up going to yoga classes, but even here the firm bodies of the other women tantalized her and made her cream in her yoga pants more than once. She knew better than to touch herself, but after another week of silence, it became too difficult. Leaving yoga class one day with an apparent wetness seeping down her legs, visibly covering her yoga pants, she made her way quickly to her car parked on the side of the street. She knew someone might see her, but it didn't matter anymore. After a second week of no release, she had to touch herself. She reached down into her yoga pants, already slimy with her juices, and began to rub her clit as people walked buy, some looking, some not seeming to notice.

The urge to cum overtook her within seconds. She had barely made three circular motions of her moistened cunt and clit before screaming loudly and convulsing in her driver's seat. Outside, a few people had stopped to stare as she collapsed into the seat and continued going. Slipping a finger into her cunt, the moisture dripped down her hand, and she continued to finger bang herself completely uncaring of the lookyloos. When she had cum again, she let out another primal scream, and a couple guys that had stayed nearby cheered her on. She drew her hand from her yoga pants, looked them in the eye, and licked her fingers clean. She wanted to invite the two men into her car, perhaps to her home, but instead started her car and drove away. She knew she wouldn't be returning to that particular yoga studio, and made her way home to shower and clean herself up.

###

The next day, Jennifer went to work as usual, stared at her boss' member as usual, and tried to understand why her Mistress had stopped contacting her. Following lunch, though, her boss approached her and told her matter-of-factly, "Jessica, Susan wants you to meet her in her office tonight."

Was it possible that Mistress knew of Jennifer's pleasure-seeking activities?

"It's Jennifer. Are you going to be there?" Jennifer asked, but raised her hands to express that she didn't really expect an answer.

"You know the drill, *Jessica.*"

###

That night, Jennifer arrived at the bar a few minutes early, dressed rather conservatively in a long dress. The bartender she had met while leaving one of her sessions with Mistress Susan was working behind the counter and immediately noticed her.

"Been awhile since I've seen you here," he said to her.

"Indeed… tell me, though, why are you always here?" Jennifer felt spirited. She knew that she may be broken later, that she may get tortured and forced to succumb to some type of humiliation, and it put a bounce in her step even though she was destined for punishment, and ultimately she may not get to climax.

"I own this place," he smiled at her. "I like to keep a watch on everything, you know? Now what can I get for you. On the house."

Jennifer blushed. That meant he knew exactly what was going on in the backroom. "Just the usual…"

"Tequila? Coming up."

No sooner had she finished taking the shot did Susan walk past her and into the backroom. Jennifer watched as she shimmied by, her luscious curves demanding every eye in the place to look towards her. There lived a coldness in her that betrayed her beauty, though.

"Go on," the bartender said. "She's ready for you."

###

Walking into the back room alone, Jennifer saw Mistress Susan setting up some items on the cart. For once, the bed wasn't setup in the center of the room. Instead, a large wooden structure was setup that had shackles attached to it and other straps.

"Clothes off," Susan barked.

"Yes, Mistress," Jennifer whimpered, lifting the dress off her head to expose her creamy skin and nude body hidden underneath.

"Stand here."

Jennifer obliged, standing in the center of the structure, a large wooden plank above her head.

"Arms up."

She lifted her arms, and Susan took the shackles from the top of the structure and attached one to each wrist. Unlatching something out of Jennifer's view, Susan then forced her arms to stretch out across the width of the plank before moving to her legs and placing each of her ankles in shackles as well. These shackles had a little space on them that allowed Susan to then place a metal bar meant for keeping Jennifer's leg's spread wide open, her dripping slit left completely exposed. Unable to move, Jennifer's exposure and situation felt dire but exciting.

"You know why you're here, yes?" Susan mouthed, not waiting for an answer. "You've been bad. I must admit, I expected it to happen much sooner, but I cannot always reward you. You must get punished or what are we even doing? Who are we?"

"Mistress," Jennifer started to speak, but Susan slapped her hard across the face. The pulsation in her cunt loved the abuse, but she felt fear.

"You didn't wear panties, so I guess I'll have to gag you with mine," Susan laughed. "Or perhaps that would be a bit too pleasing to you?"

Jennifer wanted to beg to be gagged with the Mistress' panties, but knew better. For all intents and purposes, she should act as though she was already gagged until asked a specific question.

Susan instead picked up a ball gag from the cart and proceeded to shove it into Jennifer's mouth roughly, tightening it around her face. "There will be pain, slut. You will make noise, and every time you do, you will get punished again." Susan ran her hand along Jennifer's shaven pussy, causing Jennifer to breathe in deeply with excitement. Susan smacked her across the face again.

Moving back to the cart, Susan used the wetness from Jennifer's cunt on her hands to lube a device that looked like it might be a rudimentary respirator. It became clear very soon that this would be going over Jennifer's tight coochie. A small hand pump on the end of the device was squeezed a few times and instantly the device suctioned onto Jennifer's pussy, causing it to swell. Susan pumped it a few more times and left it hanging there.

Jennifer was ready to cum already, but knew that she must hold it, that much more would come from the night and she probably wouldn't be releasing today. "You really disappoint me," Susan said. "I thought perhaps you could go a month…"

Jennifer muttered a muffled sound into the ball gag. Without hesitation, Susan grabbed a small whip from the cart and smacked it across each of her tits, leaving red marks and causing Jennifer to yelp with pain. Susan pumped the pussy pump a little more, and the swollen pussy lips became a little more engorged within the clear device before slapping her across the ass with the whip, leaving another mark.

Again, Jennifer had a difficult time keeping quiet, and Susan laughed. "Now, now, you really are a dumb fucking slut. Do you think this is fun? Are you here for joy?"

Jennifer didn't want to contemplate those types of questions. It didn't matter why she needed this treatment, and delving into it was sure to only bring up trouble.

Susan moved to the side of the installation, and with a remote attached to a large wire, she pressed a button and the chains that held Jennifer's wrists above her head tightened, lifting her off the ground, straining her arms, her legs still spread open with the spreader bar.

Jennifer let out the smallest whimper possible, and Susan once again raised her in the air just a little further. She moved back to the pussy pump, gave it a few squeezes. Jennifer's pussy lips were now completely engorged, filling out the entire area of the pussy pump, an obvious moisture building within the confines of the small area. The swelling drove Jennifer insane, she wasn't sure she could actually take anymore, and to her great relief, Susan left it be and moved back to the cart.

While Susan seemed to be working on something, the door to the back room opened and several people walked in. It appeared to be four individuals, of both sexes. As always, they were dressed in black from head to toe, with only their hands exposed. As a group, they silently approached Jennifer and stood by as she squirmed. Jennifer could see hard-ons exposed in two of the skin-tight black suits, but knew that her boss was not one of the men present this time. After all, she had spent almost two weeks staring intently at his crotch at work. But her mind raced back to her last session, the reward she received when getting double penetrated by her mistress and her boss at the same time.

"Each of you get one opportunity to inflict punishment on this harlot," Susan announced, now facing the crowd of four individuals. "As you can see, she is already lifted off the ground, her legs are spread, and her pussy has become a balloon in the pump."

Susan walked to the pump and removed it, exposing the enormous mound of Jennifer's swollen, pink pussy. A glob of her juices fell to the ground as the pump came off.

"You now, pick your poison."

Jennifer couldn't help but get excited by the group, now looking at the items on the cart and trying to decide what each of them would like to do to her. Her heart raced, and her cunt pulsated along with it, the blood very slowly moving away from the puffy pussy.

The first guest appeared to be a woman of average build, but with very perky breasts. She took from the cart a set of anal beads and a small device that looked like a magic wand. Approaching Jennifer, she caressed her puffed slit before grabbing it hard, giving Jennifer a jolt that made her squeal into the ball gag. From behind, Susan whipped her across the ass again. This time, Jennifer kept quiet.

The guest proceeded to her backside and using the lubrication from her cunt, she oiled up Jennifer's asshole and popped the first bead inside, then the second, and third, all the way up until there were six beads in her ass, filling her up to the brim. She then took the wand, and touched it to the puffy pussy... it let out an electric shock that caused Jennifer to jerk hard and let out a whimper.

Again, Susan smacked her across one of her tits with the small whip. Again, Jennifer remained quiet this time.

The guest pulled out a single bead, and shocked Jennifer again. She took in a deep breath, but remained quiet. The guest once again caressed the puffed out pussy lips, relishing the creaminess that seemed to seep out, and without warning grabbed the handle on the beads, stuck the wand in Jennifer's pussy, and electrocuted her while yanking the beads out all at once.

Jennifer's body convulsed heavily, and her scream broke the barrier of the ball gag. She had never felt so tense in her entire life, her butthole stretched and aching, her pussy feeling almost burned. With the wand coming out from her engorged mound, another stream of pussy juice fell to the ground.

Susan slapped Jennifer's ass with the whip twice, drawing a tiny amount of blood the second time, just barely breaking the skin. Jennifer barely noticed the sensation.

"Did you enjoy that?" Susan asked, not expecting an answer, but now lowering the shackles that held her just elevated in the air before lifting the shackles around her legs. Once she had finished, Jennifer lay suspended in the air in what almost looked like the missionary position.

The first guest ventured back to the cart and relinquished her items.

"You now," Susan pointed to one of the men, who had an obvious erection. He first approached Jennifer to examine her body, grope at her tits, and lifting his mask, he bit down hard on one of her nipples. Jennifer squirmed but remained quiet.

Going to the cart, he picked up several clothes pins and made his way back to her. He first placed two on each of her nipples, the pressure being unrelenting and sending electricity throughout her body. A third he placed on her clit, already enlarged and sensitive, and she let out a scream so horrid that Susan would almost cringe. Instead, she slapped her across the snatch with the whip, making sure to hit the clothes pin along the way.

Jennifer's breathing became heavy, and now tears ran down her face as the punishment for her bad behavior continued. The guest flicked on the clothes pins and bit, and then buried his face into her swollen cunt to get a taste as he began stroking himself.

"Now, now," Susan said. "If you are done punishing her, you can back away."

The guest seemed defeated but obliged the Mistress.

The third guest came up immediately following, and appeared much more confident about the events going on in the room than the previous guests. The second of the men, this guest immediately approached Jennifer without going to the array of tools. He stood at her side, and immediately wrapped his hands around her neck, choking her hard. Her face quickly turned red, and she jerked about frantically, aroused but scared, as he didn't lessen his grip. As she let out startling groans through the gag, Susan stood by and smacked the whip across her swollen lips over and over. Just before she believed she would surely black out and suffocate to death, the man lessened his grip, and backed off.

Jennifer heaved for a while, and the final guest did nothing as she caught her breath. Susan stood by, smiling mischievously just inside Jennifer's eyesight. Once the fear started to fade away, Jennifer realized that fluid was simply leaking out of her cunt now. She could hear it dripping in the silence of the room as the guests just looked on, mildly touching themselves and hidden behind their all black masks.

"Now," Susan motioned to the final guest. The final guest was obviously a woman, about Jennifer's size but perhaps a little plumper. She approached the cart, Jennifer trying to watch her as tears continued to stream down her face. The pain of all the sensations seemed to intensify as oxygen reached her brain again.

The final guest approached her puffed out slit, and without warning stabbed a small acupuncture needle into her clit, already pinched down and made sensitive by the pumping and by the clothespin. She continued to stab four or five more small needs into the puffy lips themselves, and Jennifer squirmed and grunted and continued to cry. Susan did not hit her with the whip this time, but just stroked her hair and said, "Hush now, you knew you had to be punished."

The nipples, still pinched as well, also took in needles, all the way through, tiny droplets of blood forming. Jennifer screamed out more, and finally the last guest backed off, satisfied with the pain and not interested in any of the pleasure of the event other than the punishment.

Finally the guests all stood together as Susan lowered Jennifer down, all the way to the ground, still stuck in the missionary position because of the spreading bars. She lay in a puddle of her own juices. The men had been stroking themselves, and with a nod from Susan, they approached her, removed their members from behind the black spandex they wore, and almost instantly, both of them shot their loads on her, one on the face, and one of her reddened vagina. Jennifer continued to cry, and the group stood there, seeming to contemplate what to do next.

Susan said, "Okay, undo it."

The guests, working together, removed the clotheslines, removed the needles, undid the shackles, and removed the gag in less than a couple minutes. Finally able to move, Jennifer curled up into the fetal position, still weeping but longing to jizz, lying in a puddle of her fluids.

"You will be good from now on?" Susan asked her. "You understand why you've been punished, yes?"

"Y-y-y-y-y-yes, Mistress," Jennifer blubbered. "Thank you, Mistress."

"Very well, clean your mess, lap up those fluids." Susan demanded.

Without any hesitation, but still continuing to cry, Jennifer humiliated herself by lapping up the massive amount of fluids she'd deposited on the ground. It covered her face, glistened along her body where she had laid in it, and she continued to lick until she couldn't find any obvious puddles left. Exhausted and embarrassed, she remained on all fours even after finishing.

"You may leave when you've finished cleaning up the rest of this mess," Susan scoffed, tossing the dress Jennifer wore on her, getting it dirty, before walking out of the room with the other guests without another word.

Jennifer remained on the ground there for some time,

crying, and wishing to touch herself. Wishing to reach that same amount of pain but experience the pleasure of releasing as well. When her crying finally subsided, she stood up and took the cart and all the items to the utility sink to begin cleaning up.

## #4: The Sissy and the Slave

Susan walked into the back room of the bar to find that it had been left a mess. Normally, her submissives would clean up after a session. It served as one last act of degradation, and it was a lot easier than cleaning the place herself. How could someone be expected to hoard so much power over others and also make time to clean up after them? Jennifer would have to be punished for leaving like this, perhaps even banished from the back room altogether.

There was no time now to do anything about it. Her session with Jimmy was about to take place, and she knew just the thing to make sure it got cleaned up and he felt her wrath. No sooner had she devised her plan did Jimmy walk into the room, sheepishly dressed in a skirt, a crop top, and a childish bow in his hair.

"Kendra," Susan called to him by his sissy name.

"Mistress, I have come as directed," he looked around at the room, obviously dirty, none of the tools and weapons apparently having been sanitized.

"I have a special task for you today," Susan started. "Bend over."

Bending over, it became apparent that Jimmy, known as Kendra to the Mistress, was wearing a small thong, clean shaven everywhere, and androgyny leaking from every pore of his body. Without hesitation, Susan approached the cart with the items from her last session, which were still ripe with Jennifer's punishment from the night before, picked up a buttplug, and handed it to Kendra.

"Clean it, lube it, and stick it."

Kendra obliged, first cleaning it with his mouth by licking it down.

"You may use soap," Susan chuckled, knowing full well that she set him up for this.

Kendra rose from his bent posture and walked with a sway to the sink, washed off the butt plug before using his soapy hands to lubricate his puckered hole. Returning to Susan, he bent back over, and slowly fixed the tip to the small opening of his mangina. Delicately, he began to push it in.

Exasperated, more so at her previous submissive than Kendra, Susan reached down and jammed the butt plug in harshly. Kendra let out a loud squeal.

"Now, I expect you to clean this place."

"Mistress," Kendra started.

"Kendra!" Susan slapped Kendra's ass so hard it instantly left a red mark. "Clean this place up. If the plug falls out even once, the session will be over."

Susan knew that the plug would fall out. It always fell out. Kendra's hole may have appeared tight, but it had been conditioned to loosen up with large objects inside of it. And so, Susan's plan was perfect. She would get the room cleaned and get to take off early for the night.

And as Kendra continued to clean, the buttplug eventually did pop out. Kendra quickly swooped down and shoved it back in to continue cleaning, and wondered when his mistress might tell him to leave. Perhaps she would punish him first? God, he needed to be punished.

Once the room was spotless and ready for a fresh session, Kendra sheepishly bowed in front of Susan.

"I saw it fall out, Kendra," Susan tsked. "I wanted to let you release today. I wanted to take pictures of you being a little slutty girl, the largest blackest strap on up your ass as I pounded away at you."

"Oh Mistress," Kendra squirmed at the thought of being her bitch. He lived for this shit. He loved it enough that he would walk around town dressed as a woman. Enough that he would gladly take any abuse. "I… understand."

"Now, now, come," Susan motioned him closer to her, standing next to the cart full of sex toys and whips and punishments. "Drop those panties."

Kendra obliged, and Susan grasped his member, "Such a small little clittie." His tiny dick lurched for the attention, having been hard the entire day. She stroked it a bit more before caressing his balls.

"Mistress,"

"Spread them wide," she said, squeezing his balls harder and harder, until finally he let out a squeal of pain.

Once his legs were apart, she approached the cart and brought back a metal device that clamped around his balls and his member. Attaching it, she tightened it until he once again squealed. The chastity belt device now on, Susan spit in his face and said, "Get the fuck out of here, you fucking pussy."

Kendra obliged, putting the thong in his pocket as he

left the back room.

Susan felt accomplished. She could go be a normal person for the rest of the evening. But she was still curious about why Jennifer had not cleaned up after herself. She would have to have a talk with her.

###

The night before, Jennifer had gotten the full punishment of pleasuring herself without the mistress' permission. Four people, each torturing her with needles or whips or a pussy pump. It was an intense evening that left her in shambles, crying and aching, and most of all, horny without the allowance of a release that she so desperately craved. She had started to get up and stretch her legs and arms, recovering from the shackles and spreader bar that had held her for what felt like hours upon hours. Finally feeling limber again, she dressed herself. Just before she truly began cleaning the back room dungeon, someone walked in. It was the bartender.

"I think you're late to the party," Jennifer said, almost sullenly.

"No, I wanted to wait a bit..." the bartender looked around, seeing the remnants of the puddles of lady liquid still on the floor from Jennifer's punishment.

She had licked it up, but wet spots still remained.

"Um..." Jennifer wasn't sure what to say. "I'm just going to clean up and I'll be out of here."

"I don't want to run you off," he said timidly. "You know, I've owned this bar for a long time, and Susan has rented this room. She's even offered to let me come back here while she's... uh, working..."

"You're not one of the guests?" Jennifer asked shyly. "I couldn't be sure, but I thought maybe you were. I mean, you're always here. You know what goes on."

"I don't want to get... too... too deep into anything like this... no offense!"

"Is there something you wanted then?" Jennifer felt uneasy.

"I... come out to the bar. I want to talk to you."

Sitting down at the bar, still feeling sticky from her punishment, Jennifer drank a beer with the bartender, who seemed nervous and unable to get the words he wanted to say out.

"If you want to come onto me, just do it..." Jennifer laughed. "I have to say, though, after the punishment

I got tonight, I'm not sure I wanted to get punished again so soon."

"You are beautiful, but it's not that… I wanted to warn you."

"Warn me?"

"Just listen, and then you can make your own decision. All the men that come in here for Susan are sissies and slowly, over time, they become more and more feminine. Once they're completely feminine, they all disappear within a few months."

"Okay, what does that have to do with me?" Jennifer sipped the beer. "I'm already all woman, and I don't think anything is happening to these men. I mean, Susan may be aggressive at times, but the arrangement can be ended at any time. We know what we're getting ourselves into."

"I know, but on top of that, all the women that come in disappear within a year," he said quietly. "I'm not saying that anything bad happens to them… I mean, I haven't really found out, but doesn't it seem like a strange coincidence? The same thing happening over and over?"

"I suppose so," Jennifer ran the rim of the beer bottle

across her lips. "But if you have suspicions that something is going on, why do you allow Susan to still use
the back rooms?"

The bartender didn't say anything for a long time,
acting sheepish and distracted. His nervousness was
off-putting for Jennifer, but she felt confident that he
was overreacting. People leave. People don't stay with
a back room bar mistress forever. Sissies have to find
new avenues for humiliation or they just get used to it
and it stops being exciting.

She groped his arm, "Listen, I'm sure everything is
fine."

"Jennifer, I think someone has been following you,"
he said. "I can't be sure, but I overheard Susan talking
with a stranger..."

Jennifer described her boss, and explained the situation where her boss was in on the back room, but he
stopped her short of any details... he already knew
the story. "It's not him. He's a taller man, dark skin,
never hangs around during Susan's sessions, but
seems to meet her during the day, sometimes here..."

Jennifer's heart stopped for a moment, but then her
pussy quivered at the thought of a stranger watching
her sleep at night. A stranger watching her use the

hose in her shower to get just a taste of sensation on her clit between releases. After all that had happened the night before, she was especially unsatisfied. The fear she knew she should feel didn't come, and instead she felt herself becoming horny and manipulative…

"What… what do I do? I can't go home!" Jennifer acted hysterical. "What if he wants…?"

"I'm not going to let anything happen," the bartender said.

"Should I trust you? I don't even know your name!" Jennifer stood up abruptly as if to leave.

"Wait! It's Bradon… you have to trust me!"

Jennifer stormed out, but Bradon followed behind her.

"It looks like you're the one following me now!"

Bradon followed her further down the street before finally catching up with her and grabbing her arm. "Listen to me. I want to protect you."

Jennifer stopped, looked him in the eyes, and nodded. She had never mistrusted him, though. She was ready to be defiant to her mistress once again, and went back with him to the bar as he locked up. They left, almost in pure silence, and went to his apartment.

At his apartment, he tried to set her up comfortably in his room while he slept on the couch, but she asked that they stay in the same bed together. "I'm not shy like that," she said.

"I... know, but..."

"Bradon," she caressed his leg and leaned close into him. "I'll be honest. I only came here because I really need you to fuck me."

Bradon didn't hesitate. He couldn't help himself. Never had any intention of stopping himself even though he could tell she was still gross from the night's events. He needed to taste her, and so immediately buried his head between her legs, and licked and swirled and tried his best to pace himself and remember to breathe.

She had an orgasm almost instantly, exploding her juices on his face, and convulsing like a dying deer still running after being shot. Letting out a roaring scream, she grabbed at his hair, pulling some out and causing his scalp to bleed a little bit. There was no turning back now. She would be punished again very soon.

She forced him to switch positions, and she hastily ripped off his pants, and with one hand held his boner while fondling his balls with the other as she bobbed up and down, slobbering on his dick. It didn't take much longer for him to cum, and she swallowed it almost instantly before hopping onto his lap and sliding her moist cunt onto his still pulsating member. Bouncing on his cock, it remained firm and powerful as she continued to buck into him wildly, again having an orgasm and covering his dick and balls with so much fluid it began leaking down to the floor almost instantly. Having finished again, she hopped on the bed, ass in the air.

"Fuck my ass. FUCK MY ASS!"

He didn't hesitate. He immediately jammed it into her, no extra lubrication, just the fluid from their nasty sex to keep everything wet. She screamed out in pain from the quick intrusion, but felt satiated and full and warm and happy as he pumped into her roughly, her anus tight on his cock. Without much warning, he blew a second load deep inside her asshole, pumping for another moment before pulling out and watching it drip out of her sphincter, down her leg, and onto the furniture below.

It had only been ten minutes or so, but both of them lay there pretty well spent. A few minutes later, Jennifer shot up excitedly and spoke, "I wonder if I'll get punished again."

"Susan won't hurt you," Bradon mumbled, rolling over on top of her, holding her down by her wrists.

"How are you so sure?" she giggled, sounding a bit reluctant.

"Because you're going to be my slave now."

## #5: The Slave Becomes the Master

When Bradon woke up, he realized that his arms were tied to the bed. Jennifer sat staring at him from a chair in the corner of his bedroom. He wanted to scream, but realized that the noise just muffled into the wad of cloth in his mouth tied off with a bandana.

"It is really a shame," Jennifer said. "Having to be so humiliated."

Bradon jerked about without any hope of moving, Jennifer now standing and hovering over him. In her hand, she held a thin stick, presumably from the tree in his front yard. She smacked it down hard against his naked thigh, causing him to jerk with the sting from the switch.

She proceeded to use the stick to lift up his ball sack before letting them drop. Bradon felt his member starting to pulse and ache with desire. She laughed briefly and ran the stick along the length of his member. It sprung to life, getting hard.

"You're enjoying this," Jennifer chuckled. "You thought you were so clever trying to keep me locked in here with you."

Jennifer smacked his cock hard with the switch, and he jerked in pain, his member getting harder yet. "You can end this anytime you want. All you have to do is say the word." She tossed the stick to the side and removed the gag from his mouth.

"YOU BITCH," he started in. He continued to berate her but was unable to phase her demeanor of superiority. "YOU ARE A SLAVE."

"It looks like you're the slave, honey," Jennifer smiled, stroking his cock briefly. Bradon settled down, unable to control the horniness that was overcoming him. She gripped his cock harder and harder until it began to hurt. He let out a shriek as she gave one last hard squeeze.

"You scream like a girl," Jennifer laughed. "It's up to you. You can be a good little sissy or I'll have to make you a sissy."

Bradon found himself speechless. He wanted to know where this would go. He wanted her to continue stroking his cock and treating him poorly.

"I have a treat for you, but only if you'll let me blind fold you and accept whatever comes next," Jennifer said, now sitting on the bed beside him, stroking his cock more vigorously before leaning in to give it one good suck.

Bradon just nodded, and Jennifer took the bandana that was used as the gag and tied it around his eyes.

Before he knew it, he heard someone walk into the room. "She does have a mighty small clittie," Susan said. "This is most unorthodox, I must say, Jennifer."

"It is what it is," Jennifer responded. "I'm no longer bound to any master. I hope you understand."

"Indeed," Susan agreed, approaching Bradon on the bed.

Bradon, recognizing the dominatrix that rents a room in his bar, went to speak but as soon as he did, Susan smacked him across the face hard, leaving a red mark instantly.

"Shut your dirty sissy mouth, you foul little girl," Susan snarled, grabbing his legs now. In the darkness of the blindfolded reality he found himself in, Bradon could feel shackles around his ankles. Spreader bars kept his legs wide open now, and Susan and Jennifer lifted his legs up.

"Would you like your hole pleasured, slut?" Jennifer laughed.

Bradon went to speak up but checked himself and just nodded. He did want his hole pleasured.

Without warning a lubed dildo went straight into his asshole, plunging deep and sending a shudder through his body so intense that a large stream of pre-cum ran down the length of his dick.

"We've got a weepy eye," Jennifer said.

Susan smacked Bradon across the face again. "You will not come until we say it is alright. If you do, you'll remain tied up until you can behave."

Bradon felt a tear coming out of the corner of his eye.

Jennifer pumped the dildo in and out of his asshole a few dozen times, and then the click of the door was heard again. Unable to see, Bradon wasn't sure what to expect.

"Come in," Susan said. "Our sweet little girl here is begging for some cock in her little poon."

Bradon felt the warmth of a body climb onto the bed and between his lifted legs. He knew it was a man, and he knew the intention and didn't say a word. He could stop this. He knew that. He knew that ultimately, this was all some game, and the decision was his to make.

He felt the warmth of a cock brush up against his asshole. The man's rough hand wrapped against his cock, as if using it to lift his legs up further, as the man's hair rubbed against Bradon's inner thighs. As the dick slammed into him, he let out a whimper, his dick still firmly grasped by the man.

"Do you like that, bitch?" the mysterious guest asked.

"Yes, master," Bradon whimpered. "Please don't stop."

Jennifer and Susan stood back a moment, watching as Bradon took in the massive cock, squirming and writhing in pleasure that can't be satiated without permission. Bradon held back an orgasm boiling up inside of him. He wasn't sure how long he could last, but fought hard to remember that he had to eventually get untied…

After a few minutes, the guest groaned hard and shot a huge wad of sperm into Bradon's asshole. As he pulled out, a glob of the semen came along with it, leaving behind a huge mess. The man hovered above Bradon, milking the last of the jizz out onto his lips. Bradon licked cautiously, and then fervishly.

The man left without any further words or actions. Bradon was left there naked, covered in jizz, a hard cock, and spreader bars keeping him from moving. He heard a snipping sound and then shuffling. Realizing one of his hands were now free, he removed the blindfold to find himself in the room alone. Everyone had left.

He lowered his legs finally, the muscles feeling stiff, his asshole sore, and jizz still running down his butt. He removed the other arm restraint, and sat up on the edge of the bed, the spreader bars still on his legs. Jennifer had left the key on his coffee table. Now he only had to get there to be able to get free.

His member still hard and aching, he decided instead to pleasure himself before taking any other actions.

###

"I'm sorry, Mistress," Jennifer said to Susan as they walked out of the bar's back room, the cart with them. "I..."

"I am no longer your mistress, Jennifer," Susan responded. "I am just Susan."

"What are you going to do now?"

"Nothing. The same things. I just have to find a new place. I'm sorry you went through that with Bradon, but obviously he was no match for the two of us, for you. I had no idea." Susan looked strange in her everyday clothes. Something about her was more beautiful than ever before.

"Could we be friends?" Jennifer started. "I mean, at any level… like, I'm hungry now, and wouldn't mind the company."

"No," Susan kissed Jennifer hard for a moment. "We need to go separate ways."

Susan walked off, dragging the cart behind her. Jennifer reentered the bar and going behind the counter, she made herself a drink, sipping it as she waited for Bradon to finally show up.

When Bradon finally got free from the spreader bar and cleaned himself up, he made his way to the bar to setup for the day only to find Jennifer, slightly intoxicated, sitting behind the bar.

"You…" he began.

"That is 'Mistress,' now, do you understand?"

He nodded. "Yes, Mistress."